SAGE OF LAS CRUCES

SAGE
OF
LAS
CRUCES

ROBERT H. HIGEL

PALMETTO
P U B L I S H I N G
Charleston, SC
www.PalmettoPublishing.com

© 2024 Robert H. Higel
All rights reserved.

No portion of this book may be reproduced, stored in a retrieval system, or transmitted in any form by any means–electronic, mechanical, photocopy, recording, or other–except for brief quotations in printed reviews, without prior permission of the author.

Paperback ISBN: 9798822958500

THE ROAD BEFORE ME

appeared to have a magical aura as I stood there looking across the highway. The morning heat emanating from the black asphalt was blending with the remaining coolness of the previous night's air. As I waited for the traffic to pass by me, my mind began recalling all the inconvenient events of this morning and the critical timeline for the rest of the day. Earlier this morning, I was surprised when my rental car would not start at the hotel. I had to have it towed to a garage to be repaired. The initial mechanical prognosis was that it could be fixed today, but the garage did not have the repair part in stock. The closest supplier with the repair part in its inventory was four hours away, and a special delivery was requested by the mechanic. In addition, my flight from Albuquerque, which was three hours away, was the only direct flight leaving tonight for my home in Seattle.

Several cars passed by me, creating a blaze of myriad colors: red, blue, white, and silver. Across the highway was a small neighborhood grocery store. It was in an antiquated building with a front porch deck and a wooden overhang. I thought the shaded deck would provide some relief from the warm morning sun. The parking lot in front of the grocery was not paved and was blanketed with silty sand, with some river rocks thrown along the edge of the highway. As I looked at the grocery store, my guess was that the building was probably built mid-century. It was in dire need of a coat of paint, and the red barrel roof tiles had faded to a dull orange. It was easy to surmise that traffic had passed for decades in front of this little store, and the accumulated dust and dirt from the highway had settled down on the roof line and the discolored exterior's adobe masonry. If one had taken a picture of this structure, known as Miggy's, no one could have guessed when the picture was taken. The store was caught seemingly in a time warp, frozen for decades.

The mechanic had suggested that either I should cross the street to wait at Miggy's or he would drive me into town. I had been through Las Cruces several times and had no need to go downtown. At least for now, I thought I would just wait at the grocery store, and if I got bored, maybe I'd go into town later. I was sure he would still be willing to take me into town if I asked later in the day.

SAGE OF LAS CRUCES

I knew it would be too warm soon to be standing on the roadside in the arid July sun. I studied again the shade under the overhang on the front porch. I thought it would do fine for now. I waited for another car to pass, and then I crossed the highway. As I approached the timeworn building, dust rose up around me from the sandy parking lot each time a car passed behind me on the highway. I walked up the three wooden steps leading to the front porch. As I ascended the steps, each one made its own unique creaking sound. As I stood on the deck in the shade under the overhang, I surveyed the porch, noting three high-backed wooden chairs and a table—all recently cleaned, as they did not contain the dust blanket that seemingly overlaid everything else. In each of the four front windows of Miggy's grocery, there were colorful neon signs advertising several popular beers. There were also posters promoting bargains for green beans, potatoes, and chicken by the pound. One large window sign announced all the daily specials, enticing customers to come inside for great bargains. The store seemed from the beckoning advertisements to offer a tremendous variety of grocery items.

The grocery had an inviting wooden screen door in which several parts of the screen had been patched and mended with interwoven screen. As I reached for the handle to open the door, I felt like I was being pushed forward through the entryway by the roaring traffic sounds behind me and the dust clouds created by the passing vehicles. I cautiously opened the door and looked inside. The first thing that caught my attention, oddly enough, was the ceiling. The light-colored ceiling tiles were faded from years of collective grime and cigarette smoke. Several of the tiles were water stained, evidencing that moisture had once leaked from the roof. There were also two large brown ceiling fans slowly turning that barely moved the air. The fans looked like antiques and perfectly fit the ambience of the store. The grocery was dimly lit by long, tubular fluorescent lights, some of which appeared to be encased at each end with dirt and dust due to years of neglect. I noted that there were a few bulbs that were not lit and needed to be replaced.

As I walked inside the store, I noticed the store shelves were orderly, and the walls and floor of the grocery appeared for the most part to be clean. I saw stacks of blankets with Native American designs of burnt-red-and-brown patterns. There were shelves on each side of the entryway that funneled me farther into the interior. The shelves contained all manner of vegetables and fresh produce. Farther in on the right side, there were refrigerated reach-in coolers containing an assortment of bottles of water, beer, and soft drinks. In the center of the aisle was a large round bin that contained a variety of children's toys. The bin was strategically placed to attract the attention of children. The bin had transparent sides that allowed smaller children to marvel at the many plastic toys inside. On the left side of the grocery were a refrigerated meat display counter and several more shelves containing canned goods. At the far end, the shelves culminated in a small counter that was boxed in glass. I supposed that the enclosure for the cashier was for security purposes. Above and behind the counter were stacks of cigarette boxes and signs trumpeting beer, wine, and cigarette sale prices. A small man wearing a ball cap and gray T-shirt sat quietly behind the counter. He had an amiable face and shades of a beard budding from his chin. He looked up at me momentarily and nodded with a faint smile. He then returned to looking down, and I could see he was absorbed, with a pencil in hand, in writing and erasing. I thought he was probably working on a crossword puzzle or maybe tracking his inventory.

I had not eaten anything for breakfast, and I began looking for things that I could eat. I saw in one of the glass coolers breakfast sandwiches, and I pulled one out. The white paper around the egg-and-bacon sandwich was cold. I thought the sandwich would probably taste better if heated, and I wondered if the grocer was able to do that for me. I also spied a clear bottle of orange juice, grabbed it, and moved to the counter. Near the counter were what appeared to be several day-old donuts stacked within a clear, hard plastic box. I surmised they had been there awhile, as the glaze on most of the donuts had a chalky hard coating and some of the dried glaze was beginning to flake off. I opened the plastic donut box carefully, juggling the sandwich and juice, and grabbed one. I proceeded to the counter with everything in hand, thinking this should be enough to get me going.

The man behind the counter looked up at me with a broad, welcoming smile and asked, "Anything more today, sir?"

Seeing several coffeepots behind the counter, I said, "Yes, a large cup of the medium roast coffee, please. Also, is it possible to warm this sandwich up?"

The grocer nodded and answered, "Yes, I can warm it up for you."

I watched as the grocer grabbed one of the glass coffeepots and poured the steaming hot coffee into a large Styrofoam cup. He handed me the Styrofoam cup and amiably said, "It's going to be another hot one today."

I quickly replied, "I can tell already."

The grocer smiled again and said, "I saw you walking across the highway from Diego's. If your car is being worked on and you have to wait long, feel free to sit on the porch." He chuckled to himself and continued, "It's the unofficial waiting room for Diego's garage."

"Thanks, I appreciate that," I replied. "The mechanic did recommend that I wait here as well."

The grocer partially unwrapped the sandwich and placed it in a small microwave behind the counter. I heard the soft whir of the microwave as it heated the sandwich. In less than a minute, two beeps indicated the microwave had completed its task.

After paying for the breakfast, I walked out holding the coffee in one hand and balancing the donuts, sandwich, and bottle of juice in the other. Outside I was instantly greeted by a cloud of dust that rose up from the highway as a car sped by. I turned and looked at the three chairs on the deck and decided to sit on the left side of the screen door. Each chair faced the highway and provided a direct sight line to Diego's garage. I placed my breakfast on the little wooden table alongside the chair, and with a long sigh, I sat down. I already felt mentally fatigued from the stressful morning. I had never had an automobile break down on the road in my fifteen years of business travels. I guess I had been fortunate. It was probably inevitable that it would happen sooner or later. Just a matter of time. The laws of probability.

I was resigned to eating my breakfast and just sitting and watching the cars drive by. I thought there was nothing I could do anyway to change the circumstances of the morning. It is what it is, as the saying goes. And this was not a terribly bad place to spend my day.

I took a bite out of the glazed donut, and for a second it stuck to the roof of my mouth. It was indeed a bit stale but still retained its sweet taste. I quickly washed it down with some orange juice. I now unwrapped the breakfast sandwich. It felt lukewarm but at least not refrigerated cold. Normally I tried to eat healthy, but it's hard on the road when you're entertaining clients and prospects.

My job usually put me on the road two weeks each month. The biggest benefit was that I had plenty of airline travel miles and hotel travel points. However, my wife was not enamored with the amount of out-of-town travel I had to do. I always felt really guilty leaving the house early in the morning to hit the road, leaving her to manage the household and our kids. But she juggled her time very efficiently, maintaining our household and even working part-time at a law office. Because of my business travel, eating out was sometimes challenging when I got back home. While on the road, I would eat at various restaurants offering a variety of cuisine. And when I got back home, the first thing my wife would say was always, "Let's go out to eat tonight." But having eaten at restaurants all week long, I usually found that nothing seemed appetizing. In the end, we ate where she wanted to eat, even if I had had a similar meal several times that week. It was fine by me, as it gave her a well-deserved respite, which made the both of us happy.

I looked across the highway at the garage. Diego was working under a car that was elevated on a lift. He was wearing a blue jumpsuit with a ball cap. The jumpsuit was faded and covered in grease and oil from years of use. He had seemed quite nice when I had spoken to him earlier. He'd promised the car would be ready by four thirty. If I could leave by then, I could make it to the airport in Albuquerque in time to make my flight.

Diego's car repair shop had two bays and appeared to be an old converted filling station. Places like this are easily recognizable: two garage bays, a little office, and a rectangular concrete island in front, the concrete island being where the gas pumps once stood. I watched Diego as he worked underneath the car. He was very focused as he worked, removing parts from the undercarriage and bending down occasionally to pick up a tool. The tow truck driver this morning had provided a personal testimony regarding the honesty and competency of Diego's garage. He had said there was no place better to get your car fixed around here. I took his recommendation over anything I had found that morning on the internet. And I thought that anyway, who would know better than a local tow truck driver the best place to take your car to get fixed?

I pulled out my cell phone and saw the time was ten minutes to nine local time. I looked at my weather app and saw that today's high would be 105 here in Las Cruces.

There was also some potential rainfall in the mid-to late afternoon. Given the heat forecast for the day, I decided to roll up my shirtsleeves to feel more comfortable.

Earlier I had called my wife to let her know the situation with the car and that I would hopefully still be coming home tonight. We had originally planned that she would pick me up at the airport with our two kids. If the car was ready by four thirty, as Diego had promised, our plans would still be good for tonight. I was really eager now to get home and enjoy the weekend with my family. The car issue had just made the week more exhausting.

I finished the breakfast sandwich and juice and started to slowly sip the coffee. The smell of French roast filled the air about me. I like the robust smell of coffee. I also need its caffeine in the morning to wake me up. The coffee surprisingly tasted quite good. I watched as another two cars raced by, kicking up a wave of dust that floated toward the porch, engulfing the structure.

I watched as a large, gleaming red luxury car pulled up in front of the grocery. The car was built low to the ground and appeared to be relatively new. A well-dressed elderly couple got out, slowly unwrapping themselves from the automobile. They were an elegant couple, and they seemed to be conspicuously misfit in this rough-looking environment. They proceeded up the steps, and the elderly woman, seeing me, smiled and greeted me: "Good morning."

"Good morning," I responded. "How are you folks doing today?"

The elderly man responded quickly, "Fine. Just fine. And how about you, sir?"

"Doing fine also," I said, thinking to myself that that was not exactly true, but I decided not to elaborate on the morning travails with the car.

"Good, you know it's going to be a hot one today," the elderly man said as he opened the screen door for his wife to enter. They both disappeared inside. I could hear them talking to the grocer as they shopped, and I assumed they were regulars from the tone of the conversation. The woman was asking questions to the grocer, whom she addressed as Miggy. I assumed, since the store's name was Miggy's, that he had to be the owner.

As Miggy responded to her questions, I could hear her husband fretting again about how hot it was going to be today. He said, "I am not going to go out and work in the yard today because it is just too dangerous in this heat." The elderly couple now exchanged further pleasantries with the grocer regarding watching a local baseball team and their favorite players. Their conversation seemed to indicate that there was a minor-league team in the area.

I could tell when Miggy started bagging their groceries. I could hear the sound of metal cans clinking together as they were placed in the grocery bag. Then the elderly woman wished Miggy a good day, and he in return wished the couple a good day as well.

The screen door creaked open again, and the couple walked out, each carrying a cup of coffee and a bag of groceries. The elderly man had a newspaper folded under his arm as he walked to the car.

The elderly woman turned around to look up at me on the deck and said, "Have a great day."

"Same to you," I responded. "Have a good one."

I watched as the elderly man slowly backed up the car and then shifted it into forward. As the vehicle moved forward, a cloud of dust rolled over the roof of the car and descended upon the porch. As the car sped away on the highway, I could see a few stones skipping and bouncing along the asphalt, kicking up from underneath the car.

I sat there a while reading the news on my cell phone. I went through my normal morning routine. I checked out our online bank account balance and daily transaction activity. I pulled up and read all my unread home and office emails and text messages. The events of the morning had disrupted my normal routine, but now I had plenty of time to catch up. There was nothing on the home front or work front that appeared to require my immediate attention. I was hoping that the rest of the day would be equally uneventful.

There was a news story on my cell phone that caught my eye. A man in Minnesota had driven through the front glass doors of a bakery thinking he had his car in reverse. Fortunately, he did not get hurt, and no one was injured. It was an amusing article, as the man almost drove his car entirely through the bakery. Only a large metal floor mixer used for kneading dough had stopped the vehicle.

As I relaxed back in the chair, anticipating a long day ahead, I suddenly heard a man's voice from somewhere singing a lively song in Spanish. I looked in each direction, first to my left and then up the highway to my right, to see who was singing. About fifty yards up the highway, I saw a severely bent-over elderly man slowly walking alone, singing happily out loud to himself. It struck me as odd, this poor soul walking by himself, seemingly undaunted by the traffic noise and oblivious to the vehicles whizzing past him. He entered the parking lot and trudged carefully toward the front porch. He walked with a slow, determined gait, and because he was so bent over, I figured he had led a physically hard life. Looking at the man's posture reminded me of my dad. He had worked in the construction business for many years, doing carpentry and framing houses. The hard work had taken a physical toll on his life, as evidenced by his posture and his many aches and pains.

I watched as the elderly man approached. At first it seemed that he did not notice me, but just before the first step, he suddenly stopped singing and looked up at me. At that moment a truck sped by on the highway behind him, and a wave of silty particles floated over his shape. The colloidal dust, backlit by the sun, surrounded him in a yellow-and-green aura that seemed to magnify his presence. As I looked at him, he appeared almost like an apparition, as if he had descended from some ethereal realm. I was immediately struck by his presence. Not by his physical appearance, but by his sheer determination to be standing in front of me in this frail yet mysterious state.

"Good morning, young man," he said with a firm but aged voice. "It's going to be another extremely hot day today."

"Yes sir," I instinctively responded, showing respect. "The weather seems to be a point of conversation around here this morning."

"I would imagine," he answered. "I suppose there's not a lot to talk about."

The old man reached for the stair railing, and I asked in a polite tone, "Sir, can I help you?"

He chuckled to himself. "No, son, I'll do just fine."

I watched him slowly hold the stair railing and hoist himself up one step at a time. I leaned forward on the edge of my chair, anticipating that I might need to catch him if he began to fall. I also did not want to distract him in any way that might cause him to misstep as he climbed upward. So I did not speak until he had made the final step and was firmly standing on the covered deck.

"I got to get out of this morning sun," he said in an exhausted tone as he looked about the deck. He seemed to instinctively move toward the chair that was on the other side of the door from me and asked, "I hope you don't mind my company?"

"No, I don't mind at all," I responded.

I studied the old man's clothing. He wore no hat and was wearing a faded long-sleeved shirt with a nondescript pattern. He had on a pair of heavily worn blue jeans that were frayed around the corners of the pockets. On his feet he wore well-worn and very unfashionable running shoes. His shoes had no laces but were coupled by large bands that held the shoes tightly around his feet. On the lapel of his shirt, I noted an insignia button. I recognized it as a button my uncle occasionally wore, one displaying he had been a member of the US Army.

I watched as the old man took small steps and slowly moved in front of the chair. He stopped for a moment, gradually turning his body around until he was hovering over the chair, and then carefully eased himself down to sit.

"You got a repair job over at Diego's?" he asked once fully seated.

Startled, I answered, "Well, yes," wondering how he could know that.

"I figured," he said. "Usually no one sits up here this time of morning but me unless Diego is working on their car. Young man, where are you from?"

I hesitated for a moment, as his tone was one of familiarity, like we knew each other. I answered, "Seattle. I'm here on business, and my rental car broke down."

He slowly leaned backward into the chair, looking up at the porch ceiling. He let out a short sigh. I could not tell if it was from fatigue or the feeling of successfully ending a long journey. Either way, I sensed he was now more relaxed.

He turned to me and began speaking. "My first car was a 1961 Chevrolet Impala. It was red and was a two-door Hardtop Sport." He paused for a minute as if to allow his thoughts to catch up. "You know how much I paid for it used in 1963?"

I didn't have any idea what the price of a car would have been back then, but I knew something bought that long ago could not have cost much. "I don't know. Maybe $2,500?" I asked hesitantly.

He chuckled to himself. "It was $1,600. It had white upholstered seats. A lady-killer."

"I bet," I said, amused by the old man's description of and nomenclature for the car.

I studied his face now as he looked at me. His skin had a brownish hue, and it was hard to determine if it was due to spending years outdoors, sun-worn, or if it was his natural complexion. His face had deep ridges in it, almost like mini canyons; his nose appeared to have been broken once along its ridge and appeared slightly disjointed. His ears were large and seemed to drag down from the side of his head. I thought the years had not been kind to him, and his face spoke volumes about probable hardships and stress. But his eyes were black as midnight and were bright and welcoming. His hair was almost white but was well maintained. He sat bent over in the chair now, looking up through his white bushy eyebrows at me.

"Son, you know cars didn't last long in those days. They rusted out, and the engines weren't built to last long."

I responded, "I hear that most were built not to last long on purpose—you know, like planned obsolescence. They could produce and sell more cars that way."

"Yeah, planned obsolescence," he said, sighing to himself. "Now I saw a 1961 Impala last night at an antique car auction on television go for $125,000." He raised his bushy eyebrows in disbelief. "I wish I could have kept my Impala. But no one in those days could afford to be single and own two cars. And who would have thought then the value could ever be more than $1,600?"

I nodded in agreement as he continued, "My name is Rafael, but everyone calls me Raffie." He leaned over from his chair and thrust his hand as far as he could toward me.

It was a friendly gesture that seemed quite natural for the old man.

"Raffie, I'm Paul Thomas," I said smiling. I reached out and shook his hand. "Nice to meet you."

I was amazed at the strength of his grip and the firmness of his handshake. I thought to myself that this was a nice old man who seemed pleasant and content in his current physical state in life. He didn't appear to have a worry in the world and didn't seem to be uncomfortable talking to a stranger.

"Paul, what do you do for a living?" he asked.

"I'm a commercial banker. I'm here on some business."

I watched him as he seemed to ruminate on what I had said. Then he slowly responded, "Don't mean any disrespect or trying to scare you. I've dealt with a few bankers in my lifetime. It must be a profession that wears on you." His voice began to trail off seemingly sadly, reminiscent. "Several of the bankers that I dealt with for many years unfortunately have passed. They were good people, very likable, but they could be hard negotiators. It's a good profession."

I agreed, responding, "It can be rewarding. But what I do can be very stressful. You worry a lot about getting new business and about making bad loans. I'm sure that's why you don't see many elderly bankers." I was curious now and proceeded to ask him, "What did you do, Raffie?" I felt a little uncomfortable asking him this question. I did not want him to feel I was being overly smug or disrespectful, as if my occupation had more import than whatever he had done for a living. I figured he had been retired for many years and had probably worked his whole life outdoors. But maybe I was jumping to a conclusion without knowing the facts. If my mother was here, she would caution me not to judge a book by its cover.

The old man answered slowly, looking down at the floor of the deck. "You know, after you've been retired for a while, no one ever asks that question." I watched a smile slowly creep across his face. It was a confident, amiable smile. I felt now that he was not going to be put off by my question. And as he continued to speak, I felt a little more comfortable with this likeable old man.

"When you reach my age, everyone sees you as a retired person and as nothing else," he began. "You don't get asked very often what you did in life. You're viewed as an anachronism. Somewhat old fashioned and out of date. You know, as if you are beyond your expiration date."

I smiled at his choice of words. My kids sometimes tell me that I am outdated. Their favorite comment is that I just don't understand today's world. I don't think the world has changed all that much, but maybe they have a point.

The old man now began to speak about his past. "Paul, I joined the army when I was eighteen. I served our country for four years."

Now I knew why the old man wore the army pin on his lapel. My uncle wore his army pin with much pride, and when asked about the pin, he would often tell people about his years in the service. He had served during the Korean War.

"I went to college after the military and graduated with a degree in geology."

I have to confess that his answer surprised me. I had not expected that he had attended any college. And I never would have thought he'd received a degree in the sciences. I suddenly felt ashamed that I had jumped to these conclusions. My mother's words again came back to me.

"Paul, I wanted to work for a big oil company because they paid well in West Texas." The old man raised his head slightly, looking out over the highway. His eyes narrowed as if he was visibly trying to see something in the distance. I could see the crow's-feet radiating outward from the corners of his eyes like the rays of the sun. The way he squinted his eyes reminded me of the spaghetti western cowboys I had seen in movies.

He coughed slightly and continued, "But I didn't like the work and decided to take a job as a driller, and I eventually advanced to a rig manager. I was a real roughneck, wearing a hard hat and working all day outdoors. I worked rigs all over Texas and New Mexico and Oklahoma for over ten years. And then one day a group of wildcatters approached me wanting a geologist who could also manage a rig team. They knew I worked hard and could be trusted. But they were a new company with a lot of risks."

I was right about one part of the old man's life. He had worked many years outdoors. And his weathered appearance provided corroboration for his story. The sun over time had seared in and branded every line and wrinkle in his face.

The old man coughed again and continued, "I thought about that opportunity with the wildcatters for several weeks. Did I want to leave my good, stable job to work with wildcatters?"

I was listening closely to his story now and commented, "I imagine that would be a hard decision. There's no sure thing in wildcatting."

"They were aggressively trying to get me to join their company," he continued. "They were calling me at night after work and sending me letters, and it got quite annoying after a while. I thought and prayed awhile about it and talked to my wife, and we agreed maybe the offer they provided could be improved to provide us some security. So I went back to them and said, 'I will join you under one condition.' I knew the condition I was going to ask for was probably a showstopper. I was sure they were going to turn it down. And that one condition was that I wanted to be compensated somehow for the risk I was taking with a start-up."

I understood his predicament—as a banker I dealt with commercial start-ups every day. As I sat there listening to the old man, I was becoming more engrossed now in his life story and wanted to hear more. "Raffie, I imagine they would have a problem being able to compensate you for the risk you were taking. Being a start-up, did they have any capital or cash flow?"

I watched as he repositioned himself in his chair and slowly chuckled to himself. "No, not much of either. But after a while, they relented and gave me something I hadn't expected. They agreed to give me an ownership stake in the company without my buying any stock. It was a fair number of shares. But it was still a risky proposition. At the time I had just gotten married. And it was going to be tough on us. But I took the job. It was a leap of faith. After I'd left my old job, we no longer had any stable income. My wife began working in a retail store and also took in laundry at night to make ends meet. She was a real trooper. But things did eventually change."

He looked away and lowered his voice, reminiscing about the past. "We didn't strike a trap for six months. I can still remember the day. Down around Amarillo we finally hit oil. We were down around a thousand feet, and we could hear the roar. A day like that stays in your mind forever. I still remember riding into town in my old pickup truck. I stopped at a pay phone and called Marcia to tell her the good news."

"I bet she was excited," I said, knowing that had to be a life-changing event. The old man's story was getting to be even more interesting, and again I wanted to hear more.

"Yes, Marcia was very excited. When I got back into town, we celebrated at a restaurant we'd thought we could never afford in a million years. Those were heady times."

"And you had an ownership stake!" I said, understanding the largesse that would have been coming to him.

"Yes, I did, Paul."

"Wow, Raffie," I said, smiling, "that was a good decision on your part to take the risk. And I'm sure you did quite well after that."

"Yes, very well," he said in a humble, subdued tone. "We struck oil many times after that. Some small strikes and some really big strikes."

As a banker, I often had opportunities to talk to many successful entrepreneurs and business owners. It was always fascinating to me to hear how a financially successful person made their fortune. Usually, it was from humble beginnings and extreme sacrifices that blossomed into greater, sometimes unexpected, rewards.

"What did you do then?" I asked, trying to encourage him to tell me more about himself. "Did you retire?"

"No, I did not retire. It is true that neither Marcia nor I needed to work anymore, but I couldn't just do nothing. I was in my thirties. I stayed on the job and kept the drillers on schedule. I continued selecting the drilling locations in our oil fields. I have to say God blessed us immensely."

"So how many years did you do that for?" I asked.

"About ten years. Then one day our company was approached by one of the major oil companies, and they gave us an offer we couldn't refuse." He chuckled to himself.

"So then you retired?" I asked inquisitively.

"No, I worked for them a couple of years," he responded. "It was a good job, and it gave me a purpose in life. Then I heard about all the oil leases that were being given out up in Alaska. And I figured Alaska was like the Southwest, just colder, with more forest land. So I decided to start my own company."

"Really?" I said, thinking this was a bold move on his part. He didn't need to take on any more risks in his life. As he'd said, he didn't need the money. So what drove him to take another financial chance in life that could end poorly?

As the old man had been speaking, his voice had maintained a calm tone. He showed very little emotion or excitement. He was not boastful or pretentious or arrogant in any way. He seemed to me to be very humble and appreciative of his good fortune. I was beginning to feel an amiable bond with this man and an admiration for what he had accomplished. It is rare to find someone who is truly successful with such humility in the world today.

"So I went up to Alaska," he continued in a calm tone. "I brought a great group of guys with me that I had worked with over the years. An all-star team of hard workers. And they got paid well for their hard work. Then, in a short time, I got an oil lease on some land and bought derricks, drill pipes, Kelly drives, blowout preventers, and everything else we needed. I had three crews working night and day in freezing weather north of the Arctic Circle. At first, we didn't strike anything. Nothing. But then the last week we could work that first season, we got a glimmer of hope. We were seeing pressure readings that told us we might be on to something big. But it was right at the time the spring temperatures were rising, and the ice roads and pads were beginning to melt."

He stopped and looked at me through his thick white eyebrows. "Do you know the most exciting thing in the world to be anticipating? Anticipating, but not knowing for certain?"

"If you struck oil?" I said, thinking he was asking a rhetorical question.

"Yes, Paul, it's when you realize you may have a large strike, but you can't stay to find out. You have to leave the area before you can't get out. In the late spring, the few roads up there become inaccessible as the ice begins to melt. The solid ground and ice become mud and slush. You can't get trucks in and out, so you have to stop drilling and wait for the ground to dry out a little more or freeze again. We had to wait a few months to return to the drilling site. The anticipation was incredible." He chuckled to himself.

"So how did it turn out?" I asked eagerly. "I assume you struck oil?"

I watched as a slowly broadening smile appeared across the old man's face. "It was a huge strike," he began. "We pumped a lot of oil from that area, and I mean a lot. And the wells we hit were productive for many years. Some are even producing today."

"Wow, Raffie, what a tremendous story," I said with excitement in my voice. "It seems like you made all the right moves at the right time."

"Not always. Trust me, I've made plenty of mistakes," the old man responded, looking down at his hands. "Paul, please don't ever think you won't make mistakes in life. That's how you learn. Too many people are afraid to do things in life because they're afraid of making mistakes or afraid of failing."

SAGE OF LAS CRUCES

*****

 A few minutes later, a white late-model car pulled up in front of the grocery. I looked down and saw a middle-aged woman and man inside the car. They sat there for a few minutes without opening a door. They appeared to be quarreling, using wild arm gestures as they spoke. I could hear their muffled voices from outside the closed car.

 Finally, the man got out of the driver's side of the car. He was slender. He was wearing a pressed long-sleeved dress shirt and a pair of khakis. I watched as he leaned back into the car and said loudly, "Lisa, you didn't want to stop for breakfast, and now you're hungry! Why didn't you eat before we left home?"

 The woman now opened her door and got out. She was wearing a smart-looking red dress and high heels. She raised her voice over the roof of the car. "You were in such a hurry to leave I didn't have time to eat. And now I'm hungry!"

 The man shut his door loudly, and the woman walked ahead of him, saying, "You can be such a jerk sometimes!" She proceeded up the steps and seemed to ignore the two of us sitting there. "Husbands!" she lamented in exasperation to herself as she opened the screen door and went inside.

The man looked up at the two of us as he approached the screen door. He appeared somewhat embarrassed. He shook his head in frustration and simply uttered an "Urrrh."

Once both were inside the store, I could hear they were continuing to bicker. They were now arguing over the food to purchase. "I thought you weren't hungry!" she said to him with a defiant tone in her voice.

"Well, if we are here, I might as well grab something to eat. Do you have a problem with that?"

"No, I don't care if you want something to eat," she responded. "But Tom, you know how upset your stomach gets eating fried food in the morning."

"Lisa, come on." The man seemed to suddenly become contrite and added, "Let's just get a bite and go. The kids expect us by two o'clock. We don't want to miss little Hudson's party."

"That would be a big mistake if we miss his first birthday party," she said in a calmer voice.

As the couple returned to their car, they both appeared to be in better moods and were even cordial, smiling at each other. I was amazed at how the initial fiery encounter had been transformed into this seeming state of mutual serenity. The couple got back in the car, and I could see them conversing inside the car, laughing. They slowly backed up onto the road and left in a morning fog of dust.

Raffie watched as the couple left, turning his head to follow their car down the road. "You know something about that couple? They will be married the rest of their lives."

I was pondering his comment and asked, "How do you figure?"

The old man looked down again at his aged hands, and I noticed the bent joints in several of his fingers. "Because any couple who can fight like that and reconcile that quickly will stay married a long time. Their love extends beyond their petty disagreements." I could tell his words were spoken from experience and wisdom.

The old man coughed slightly again and turned toward me and said, "Marcia and I had many arguments, but we stayed married. She even followed me to Alaska and lived like a trooper in the wilderness when she could have lived anywhere on this earth."

What he said prompted me to ask a question I had been thinking about. "Your wife must be a very special woman. I don't think I could get my wife to live in the wilderness in Alaska. No matter what I promised her."

I could see the old man's countenance droop a bit. He looked straight ahead at the highway, and I could see his eyes moisten amid the dry exterior of his face. "Fifty-five years we were married," he said proudly. "We had a great marriage and understood each other. We raised two fine kids. But my Marcia passed away two years ago after being sick for some time."

I could tell the old man was still in grief from his wife's passing. He grew silent for a while, and I attempted to provide a comforting response. "I'm sorry to hear that. It sounds like she was a great woman and a great partner in life. I'm sure it's hard to lose someone you've lived with that long."

He turned away from me, hiding his face, subtly wiping his eyes with the back of his hand. I knew not to say anything more and to allow him to grieve quietly. After a while he turned back around and looked at the ground for a second or two and then added, "It is tough to lose someone who knows you better than anyone else ever could. Someone you truly love. We always supported each other, and we worked together as a team."

*****

The sun was slowly rising in the morning sky, and the shimmering mirage created by the heat rising from the asphalt was beginning to blur Diego's garage across the street. It was a dry, arid heat that I was not accustomed to. In Seattle we have moderate to cold wet weather mostly year-round. I wondered if I could ever live in a place like this.

The warmth of the morning did not seem to affect Raffie as he sat leaning forward in his chair. I could see the aging arch of his back clearly as it curved up from the back of the chair. I could only imagine how many countless times his back had been called upon to lift heavy oil rigging, piping, or metal pipe chains. The heavy lifting had undeniably taken its physical toll on his body, but he did not seem to be in any pain or discomfort.

A vehicle pulled off the highway and stopped abruptly in front of the porch. It was a faded red minivan that was well past its prime. The right front tire had a smaller and thinner temporary wheel that, if I could judge from the condition of the tire, had been on the van significantly longer than intended. There was a sticker on the bumper showing a view of Grand Canyon National Park. I noticed several scratch marks on the hood. I could see that an effort had been made to cover some of the scratches with red paint. The touch-up paint unfortunately didn't quite match the original faded paint color. And in some places the touch-up paint was chipping off.

A young woman opened the driver's side door, which made a metal creaking sound. As she got out of the van, she admonished a child I could see wiggling back and forth in a car seat. "Now wait till I get you out, Henry. Just sit still."

She walked around the front of the van. She was slim and dressed in faded jeans and a white T-shirt. Her hair was jet black and in need of a good brushing.

She opened the front passenger side door and began unbuckling a child from a car seat. "Henry, sit still. I need to unbuckle you first. Stop. Henry, be still." She lifted the boy and placed him on the ground beside her. She took his hand and walked him to the front of the van.

She admonished the little boy with an ominous, stern warning: "Now stand here, Henry. Do not move until I get your sister out, understand?" The little boy nodded his head in obedience.

As she proceeded to open the van's side door, the little boy stood motionless, looking at the ground. He glanced up at us on the porch, and when he saw that we were watching him, his eyes quickly darted back to the ground. Feeling he was under our gaze, he began moving his feet slowly in the sand. And then he began to fidget and slowly walked toward the other side of the van. At that moment his mother appeared, carrying an infant, and caught the little boy by the arm, pulling him in front of her.

"Henry, I told you to stand in front of the van." She spoke sternly. "You never listen. Let's go inside. We need to get some groceries for dinner."

She walked past us without speaking. She was preoccupied with corralling Henry and holding the infant to her shoulder. Up close, I could see she wore no makeup, and she appeared very tired looking, with dark lines under her eyes. Once she went inside the grocery, the little boy could be heard moving about and shuffling his feet on the wooden floor.

"Mommy, can I have this?"

"No, Henry, we are only going to buy food. No toys today. Daddy is not paid until next Friday."

The boy pleaded, "But Mommy, my bulldozer broke. I need a new one."

"Henry, what did I say?" She raised her voice. "You are not listening. We are here to buy food. Do you want to eat tonight?"

The boy persisted. "But Mommy, my birthday is coming up. Can't I have this?"

The mother responded, "No, Henry, we can't spend any more money right now."

The woman now began asking questions of Miggy. I could hear the conversation through the screen door. "We came here because we heard you run specials sometimes," she said. "We live outside of Rincon. What do you have on sale today?"

Miggy answered, "Well, ma'am, we have black beans, red beans, green beans, and rice on sale today. Also, we have eggs and some chicken and bacon at a real good price.

The chicken just came in on the truck this morning. It's real fresh."

The woman sighed. "Well, how much are pinto beans?"

"Today they are fifty cents per can or seventy cents for dried. Ma'am, that's a good price."

The woman's voice hesitated. "How much are the red beans?"

Miggy responded, "Well, they're seventy-five cents per can."

Suddenly the boy spoke up. "Mommy, why can't you buy me that bulldozer? Mine is broken. It could be my birthday present."

"No, Henry," she said, scolding the little boy. "When I'm talking to this man, do not talk to me. And quit asking for something you are not going to get."

As the woman continued talking to Miggy, the boy suddenly appeared at the screen door, looking outside. He stood there very quiet and very solemn. I could see out of the corner of my eye that he was staring at the van outside. At that moment Raffie turned toward the screen door, and seeing the little boy, he turned back around and began studying the ground in front of him. I could see in the old man's eyes that he was thinking of what to say or do.

Raffie began to slowly turn sidewise in his chair, and he began to wrestle with something in his back pocket. A few seconds later, I could see that he was holding a rather worn leather wallet. I watched as he opened the wallet, and I saw quite a few bills neatly stacked in the fold. He fumbled, with great difficulty extricating just one of the bills. I could see it was a crisp new ten-dollar bill. He turned slowly in his chair and knocked on the screen door to get the boy's attention. In a quiet, whispering voice, he told the boy, "Here, son, give this to your mother and tell her she can buy the toy you want."

The boy opened the door slowly and hesitantly as he took the bill in hand. He softly said politely, "Thank you."

I could hear the shuffling of small feet along the grocery floor as he walked back toward his mother. Suddenly his mother quit conversing with Miggy and said in a loud voice, "Henry, where did you get that money from?"

The boy meekly responded, "The older man out front. He said you could now buy the bulldozer toy for me."

Her voice now went into an even louder scolding tone. "How many times have I told you not to take money from strangers? Where is this man?"

I could hear them walking on the wooden store floor back toward us. The screen door opened abruptly, and the woman appeared with the infant on her shoulder. "Mister, did you give my son this money?" she asked accusingly, looking at Raffie.

Raffie looked up at her sheepishly and nodded, acknowledging her objection. He meekly responded, "Yes, I did give him the money. Ma'am, I'm very sorry. I know I should have asked you first."

The mother seemed to ignore Raffie's apology and continued in a harsh tone, "You may have thought this was a good thing. But I have been teaching Henry not to take any money from strangers. It's a lesson we do not break. It's a matter of protection, and if I make an exception, he won't learn the right thing to do. Mister, we don't have much, but I want to raise our son right."

Raffie was silent and sat listening. He nodded slowly in agreement, and his head bent down farther, and in his eyes, I could see he felt he had committed a wrong and felt remorseful.

"Henry, give the man back the money," she demanded. "We do not take money from strangers."

The little boy timidly handed the bill back to Raffie, not letting the bill go until Raffie firmly had the bill in hand. "I'm sorry, son. You need to listen to your mother. She is a wise lady and only wants to protect you."

The mother's voice softened now and said, "Mister, I know you were trying to help. Don't take my harsh words the wrong way. It's just been a bit overwhelming for us of late."

The mother and son turned and went back inside the store. She began conversing with Miggy again about the price of goods. Raffie sat quietly looking down at the deck, still stinging from the scorn of the boy's mother. He did not move, and after a short time he finally raised his head and called out, "Miggy, Miggy." I was amazed at how loudly he could project his voice, speaking at a volume I thought he was incapable of reaching.

A voice came from within the store. "Yes, Raffie. What do you need?"

"Would you say we had three hundred days of sunlight last year?"

Miggy responded slowly, "Yes…I would think that is about right."

"Good, I thought so."

Then the old man paused and appeared to be recalculating his estimate for a moment and again raised his voice. "No, Miggy, I think it was more like three hundred fifty days of sunlight last year."

"Yes, Raffie, that is probably better."

I could hear Miggy addressing the woman as she finished her shopping and was ready to check out. "You know, ma'am, you came here for sale items. I do have a box of fifty cans of black beans, several twenty-pound bags of rice, some loaves of bread, some chicken, some beef, bacon, eggs, corn, green beans, bananas, and milk that I have to get out of the store today. I have another shipment coming in. I can promise you the food is very fresh, and I need it moved out to free up more shelf space. You would be doing me a favor if you took it."

The woman did not answer right away. Then she slowly asked, "How much would that cost?"

Miggy hesitated. "Well, again, you'd be doing me a favor taking the produce and food. I could let you have it all for twenty-five dollars."

The woman responded in a surprised tone, "Twenty-five dollars? I don't know what to say. Really? Just twenty-five dollars? And you said it's all fresh. Well…well, thank you, sir." I could hear the woman's voice start to soften again, and she continued with an appreciative tone. "Sir, this is very nice of you to offer this to us. Are you sure this is OK?"

"Ma'am, it is OK. I have to get it out of the store today. Let me start getting it together for you."

I could hear Miggy quickly rustling up a shopping cart. The cart's wheels squeaked as he pushed it around the store, gathering the food into it. I thought to myself, that if only I had a spray can of lubricant, I could stop the annoying squeaking of the wheels.

As Miggy loaded the cart, he would ask the mother whether she would like some of this or that. She would answer in an appreciative tone, "If that is OK with you, sir." At other times, Miggy wouldn't ask and would just say she needed this or that and put it in the cart. It took about twenty minutes for Miggy to get everything loaded. Then I could hear the cart being pushed toward the screen door.

At the screen door, I heard Miggy tell the mother, "Ma'am, one more thing. I have put something special in a plastic bag for you labeled 'Later.'" Then he lowered his voice so as not to be overheard by the little boy. "Let your son open that bag later."

Miggy opened the screen door, pushing and pulling two fully loaded shopping carts stacked with a cornucopia of fruit and vegetable cans, milk cartons, loaves of bread, bags of fresh vegetables, stacks of frozen chicken and beef and pork, large bags of rice, and many other canned staples. Additionally, he went back inside and came out carrying three egg cartons, each carefully separated in its own brown paper bag.

I watched as Miggy carefully pushed each cart down a ramp on the side of the building. Once he was in the sandy parking lot, I could see the tracks of the wheels in the dirt as he pushed the heavily laden carts to the rear of the van. He placed the food stock gingerly in the back of the van, carefully avoiding hitting his head on the rear raised hatch, as it did not extend to its appropriate height. He was grouping and placing the items in neat rows so they would not roll around in the back of the van. The woman had placed Henry in the front car seat now and was still holding the infant to her shoulder. "Sir, I really thank you for all this," she said in disbelief and appreciation. "I wasn't asking for anything special. But bless you. I really appreciate all this, and I don't know what else to say other than thank you."

Miggy smiled and nodded. "Ma'am, no problem. I will put these egg cartons on the floor of the front seat to keep them safe. I appreciate you doing me this favor in opening my shelf space." Miggy lowered his voice now and said, "And this bag here, remember—let your son open it up later."

Almost instinctively the woman leaned forward and gave Miggy a hug. "Thank you again so much. Sir, this is so kind of you."

I watched as the mother placed the baby back in the car seat and got inside the van. She backed up onto the highway cautiously and drove away. I could see the little boy in the back seat sitting quietly, looking at us with an expressionless face.

As Miggy walked back to the porch, I noticed he looked at Raffie and nodded.

*****

A steady stream of cars and trucks whizzed past the store all morning, each time kicking up more dirt and silt from the side of the road. Many patrons had come in and out of the store. The morning had kept Miggy very busy.

Several folks were regulars and fondly greeted Raffie on the porch. He seemed to enjoy talking to the regulars and did not seem tired in the growing fieriness of the day.

After the morning bustle was through, the old man sat back and just watched the cars pass on the highway in front of us. I kept thinking how nice it was of Miggy to help that young woman out, and I finally broke the silence. "How long have you known Miggy? He seems like a good friend of yours."

Raffie slowly turned to me and answered, rubbing his chin, "We go back a few years. He was the first person I met when we moved here. I know his family very well. They are all good people."

The old man turned his focus now toward the street, and I watched his eyes open very slowly, like those of an old sea turtle I had once seen in Florida. "I met his dad in boot camp. We were both stationed at Fort Sill coincidentally. His dad passed away several years ago." The old man continued with the story, saying, "I went to 'Nam after that in sixty-three as part of an early presence. Stayed off and on for three years in 'Nam." The old man lowered his voice as if remembering something that had happened a long time ago that he wished he had forgotten. Something that brought back forbidding memories. "You know, Paul, I almost didn't make it back from 'Nam."

I watched Raffie as he began to recall a different time in his life. His voice was very methodical as he spoke in a measured tone. "I don't tell this story much," he slowly began. "Our platoon was camped along a river in country on an extended sweep. We encountered the enemy twice and had some small firefights. One night we camped near a river. It was so hot that night, and some of us young bucks jumped in the river to cool off. I guess we also took in some water. I got really sick and had to be airlifted out with several of my platoon members. I had a bad internal bacterial infection, and it later was determined that the Viet Cong had mutilated livestock upstream to punish a village for cooperation with our soldiers. They had dumped several animals in the river and even a few village people. All that decaying matter came downstream."

The old man stopped and looked at me to make a point. "You know, regardless of what anyone thinks about that war, I am very proud of my service in Vietnam. Maybe we shouldn't have been there. Or at least should have fought the war differently. It was the politicians and military brass that screwed up our efforts. A lot of young men lost their lives, and it could have ended sooner with better results."

I did not interrupt or speak, as it appeared Raffie was trying to find the right words to continue. I was intrigued by Raffie and his life, and I wanted again to hear more of his life's story.

"There were a lot of unsung heroes over there," he continued. "But the true heroes were the servicemen and women who gave their lives. I had friends I think about often who didn't make it back." He paused for a moment in silence and looked down. Then he spoke with conviction in his voice. "Paul, I disagree on one point about that war. There was a noble cause. We were fighting to stop the spread of communism and socialism. The Russians and Chinese were indoctrinating citizens in various countries at that time with their promise of an economic utopia and great society. Only brutality and tyranny result from that type of economic system."

The old man turned now, and he looked at me through his thick white eyebrows. His forehead furrowed. "Do you know who was responsible for killing the most people in the twentieth century?"

I had heard the answer to this question in high school. I responded, "I don't think it was the Nazis."

"No, as evil and vile as they were, it was not them," Raffie answered. "It was the communist Chinese and then the Soviet Union. I think today most people would be surprised to hear that. The evils of totalitarianism are always driven by people with excessive egos and with perceived good intentions. This is why democracy must always prevail. We can change our leaders."

*****

As we sat there, an old pickup truck sped by us with an American flag lodged on the side of the tailgate. As the truck passed, the unfurled flag flapped in the wind. I saw that Raffie was watching the truck as it drove down the highway, disappearing in the distance.

He slowly turned back toward me and said, "I like to see our flag displayed. It does bother me when individuals disrespect our flag or national anthem." The old man spoke with a growing annoyance in his voice. "There are many ways to protest in this country. And no one will stop you. But don't disrespect the flag. It may have had fewer stars, but that same flag was raised on Iwo Jima. That same American flag was raised at Gettysburg. That same flag flew over Pearl Harbor. That same flag flew over the rubble of 9/11. It is our rallying symbol that we are Americans and are together in unity. To break that symbol is to break the unity of the brothers and sisters who fought for this country and who work every day to keep it going." He stopped, and his voice grew bolder. "Men and women risked their lives for this country, and some gave it all, including their lives, for that flag."

I could tell this was a point of no compromise of values with the old man. He continued talking in a bold tone, "If you dishonor our flag and national anthem, you are showing disrespect to those that served and fought and to those that didn't make it home. And that includes those that fought and became physically and mentally disabled as well. We would not be free today and be able to freely express our differences without the sacrifices they made."

He stopped again, lowering the intensity of his voice to make a point. "In this world, if you want respect, you have to be respectful. Defying the flag is not respectful. If you wish to protest your discontent, do it in other ways. Our country's hard-fought freedoms give you the right to peacefully protest."

I nodded in agreement, understanding his fervor, and said, "Raffie, I believe disrespecting our flag or anthem only leads to being disrespected. It seems to me that you don't win your point by offending people and being disrespectful. I mean, you fought for this country, and so did my dad. I am very appreciative of people who serve. Really, you are all patriotic heroes."

"I'm not a hero," the old man quickly responded. "I was doing my job. As I said, the servicemen and women who lost their lives or who were disabled while defending this country are the true heroes."

*****

It was just past ten thirty now, and the earlier long shadows that had stretched out toward the highway had partially retracted. The old man called out to Miggy. "Miggy, in about an hour, when you have some time, will you please bring us two large bottles of water and two of your famous ham-and-cheese sandwiches for lunch?" He then turned to me and said in a quieter tone, "Paul, is that all right by you?"

"Yes, that's fine," I answered, thinking I had no better place to have lunch than here.

I could hear Miggy inside conversing with his many customers. He greeted everyone cordially, and it sounded like he truly enjoyed talking to his patrons. At this time of day, most of his customers were there to get their midmorning nourishment and a break from their early-morning work. Most of Miggy's clientele were working men that appeared to be field workers or in the construction trades—workmen like plumbers, electricians, framers, and ranch workers. They were usually younger. The few older men among them usually walked slowly and sometimes hobbled side to side. The older men all had weathered appearances. All seemed to be driven to this oasis for refreshment and a short respite from their morning's arduous work.

After the last of the early lunch crowd had departed, the screen door opened, and Miggy came out onto the porch.

He handed each of us a sandwich neatly wrapped in white paper and a large bottle of water.

"Here you go, gentlemen," he said with a broad smile. "Anything else, Raffie?"

"Nothing more for me," Raffie replied, and then, turning to me, he asked, "Paul, do you want anything else?"

"Nothing more for me either. This will do fine. Thank you."

Then, turning to Miggy, the old man said in an appreciative tone, "Then I think we are set. Thank you, Miggy."

I watched as Raffie slowly unwrapped the sandwich, which had been sliced at an angle into two pieces. He lifted the sandwich to his mouth, and I could see a sparkle in his eyes as he took the first bite.

"That's a good sandwich," he said, nodding his head approvingly. "The bread makes it. Miggy gets it fresh each day from a bakery downtown. The cheese is imported smoked gouda. You can really taste the smokiness."

As I unwrapped my sandwich, I picked up the deep scent of smokiness, and I could feel the softness of the bread. The first bite confirmed Raffie's approbation. "Very good," I said. "The bread is excellent. Real fresh. I like the spiciness of the peppers as well. The jalapeños give it a good kick."

The old man turned to me and jokingly said, smiling, "I hope you can handle the peppers. They really make the sandwich. Down here we don't eat bland food."

After taking a drink of water, trying to lower the heat in my mouth, I turned to Raffie and inquired, "How much do I owe Miggy or you for the food and drink?"

The old man shook his head abruptly and answered, "Nothing. It's taken care of."

I insisted, "I owe one of you some money. You know I'm here on a business trip. It doesn't come out of my pocket. Can't I at least pay for my sandwich? I mean, I feel I owe someone something."

The old man answered, "No, that's fine. I enjoy your company. And Miggy gets paid. He just puts it on my tab."

"Well, Raffie, thank you for lunch. I appreciate it."

*****

As we finished our sandwiches, a bright red sedan pulled up, and a smartly dressed middle-aged woman got out of the driver's side of the car. She was carrying a laptop case and had a set of rolled building plans under her arm. The old man looked up, and seeing her, he began to smile before she spoke.

"Mr. Raffie, how are you today?" she greeted him. "I'm so glad we can meet today on such short notice."

"No problem," Raffie answered agreeably, nodding his head. "Margie, this project is very important to me. I want to make sure it is very successful. I'm glad you are available as well to discuss this."

The smartly dressed woman ascended the stairs and approached Raffie, extending her free hand to shake his. He stood up and greeted her, reciprocating the handshake. He motioned toward the chair next to him. "Margie, please sit here. I see you came prepared."

She sat down in the chair and exhaled deeply in a sign of excitement. "Well, I hope you are having a great day, Mr. Raffie. I have the architect's renderings here on my laptop, and I've got a draft of the site layout we can review today. I just want to say again that the committee is very appreciative of your effort to build the sanctuary for women suffering from domestic violence in our community. It will help many women and their children."

I watched as Raffie's smile began to dissipate and a serious, concerned look came upon his countenance. "Margie, this is so important to this community and to the women that have no place to go for safety. As you know, my sister suffered from domestic violence. I saw first hand how difficult it was for her and her children. I feel I am called to help others who suffer from domestic violence like my sister and have no place to go. This is something I personally feel is needed, and I am honored that I'm able to help this cause."

"Mr. Raffie, we are honored as well."

Margie opened her laptop and with a few keystrokes turned the laptop toward Raffie so he could see the screen. "Now this is the layout you approved last." I watched as she motioned toward the screen, describing several key points. "As you know, we approved three apartment buildings and a community center featuring a communal kitchen, a playroom, an education center, and counseling rooms. Building one here is for women that have no children, building two has two-bedroom apartments, and building three has three- and four-bedroom apartments."

I watched as Raffie slowly nodded. He was intently studying the screen and rubbing his chin. "Margie, there will be security around the structures, right?"

"Oh yes, we will have a seven-foot fence around the buildings and cameras throughout the common areas and outside the buildings. We will have a night watchman, and the county has agreed to post an officer at night and throughout the day near the entrance for further security."

"Good, good," Raffie responded. "And how many children do we expect will be on-site at any one time?"

"We have thirty apartments in total. So I would estimate we'll probably have between thirty-five and fifty children at any one time."

Raffie motioned toward the rolled plans resting against the side of her chair. "Margie, do you mind showing me the layout on the site plans you brought?"

"Of course not. That's why I brought them with me for you to review."

Margie unrolled the plans that she had placed beside her chair. "Mr. Raffie, here is a draft rendering of the layout of the buildings within the fencing. You can see all the buildings and common areas."

The old man pointed to a section on the plans. "This is the playground for the children here. And I see you've divided it between a place for smaller children and a section for older children. I like that."

Suddenly Raffie turned toward me and said, "Margie, here is a friend of mine, and I want to ask his opinion on the size of the playgrounds. Paul, I suppose you have children. Do you think this area should be expanded for the smaller children?"

I was caught off guard and at first hesitated to answer. I was not expecting to be brought into this decision process, but Raffie was looking at me for earnest input. "Well, yes, I do have children, and they do like to spend a lot of time on playgrounds. I would say this will be a major part of their daily enjoyment. It may be their principal outdoor activity, other than at school. I would make it bigger."

Margie nodded. "I agree with Paul. Children have to be children. Giving them more play space would be a nice improvement."

Raffie slowly nodded as he contemplated our input. "Can we do that, Margie? Make this change?"

Margie began to smile wryly as she looked at Raffie and me. "Well, yes, Mr. Raffie—it's your prerogative. You are paying for all this. We can do anything you want us to do."

"Good, then let's do it. Please make that change."

Margie smiled again and said, "Consider the change made. We'll add a few more swings and a playground system with more overhead shade shelters to keep it cooler. Is there anything else you wish to change?"

"Well, let me see. How do the children get to school?"

"The county has agreed to place a bus stop in front of the center. There will be a bus for the elementary school children and one for the middle schoolers."

"That will be convenient for the mothers and their children," the old man responded. "I do have another idea I've been thinking about that will provide these families some needed time together. Are there any planned field trips or fun things the mothers and children can do off-site? Are there plans for an activity bus?"

Margie hesitated at first and then calmly responded, "We don't have that in the budget. We are getting funding from both the county and the city, as well as several local businesses. And we have three thrift shops now that will help fund the facility when it's completed."

The old man nodded slowly. "Let's add an activity bus so the women and their children can go out after school. Especially in the summer when the schools are out and they can do fun things together. You know, that's very important. Just add a twenty-seat bus to the construction costs."

"Well, thank you," Margie responded effusively. "It's so nice of you to add that. It will make a lot of mothers and their children very happy. We already have a volunteer who has a license to drive a bus and has expressed an interest in helping us. And we have other volunteers to coordinate and manage these outside activities."

"One last thing, Margie. I know we discussed this during our last meeting. Is there any faith-based help for some of these women and their children? I know you were working on this."

"Yes, I'm glad you brought that up. Several churches have expressed an interest in providing worship services on Sunday afternoons and evenings as desired. It is strictly a voluntary program."

"Great. Thank you for working on that." Raffie leaned back in his chair now, and I noticed across his countenance an ease of contentment and satisfaction. "Well then, Margie, that's all I have as far as input and changes. Are we still shooting for a late-fall opening next year?"

"Yes, that is still the goal."

"Margie, I want to thank you again for meeting with me on this. I appreciate everything you are doing to make this happen. Are we still scheduling monthly update meetings?"

"Yes, the next meeting I have on my calendar is the fifteenth of next month. We can meet here again, same time, same place."

"Fine by me. I can't wait to visit the center when it's completed."

Margie smiled and replied, "Mr. Raffie, you will be the first visitor before it's officially opened. Without your commitment and continued support, this project would never have gotten off the ground. Thank you again."

Margie stood up now and gave the old man a side hug and another handshake while holding her laptop and the plans. "Have a great day, Mr. Raffie. You are doing something very good for this community."

*****

Shortly after the noon hour, Miggy's business picked up again. Flatbed trucks carrying construction materials and work trucks containing laborers constantly pulled off the highway into the dusty parking lot. Sometimes big SUVs pulled up, and groups of men piled out to get some nourishment before returning to work. I watched them as they walked by us, many acknowledging Raffie and greeting him with respect. Raffie would inquire how their days were going or how their mothers or fathers were doing. Several of the men he knew quite well from the community and church events. He would joke in Spanish with them and laugh at their responses. He seemed to enjoy the attention and banter.

A large plumbing truck pulled up with white PVC pipes of all sizes stacked on top, along with elbows and fittings hanging from the side. Four men slowly got out and stepped up onto the porch. One man wearing a faded yellow T-shirt with "Hayden Plumbing" emblazoned across his chest stopped at the screen door and did not go inside. He loitered on the porch and waited for the rest of his coworkers to enter the grocery. I watched him as he stood beside Raffie, and then he suddenly began speaking to him furtively, in a hushed tone.

"Sir, if you have a minute, can I ask you for advice?" he asked timidly. His face projected a concerned and earnest look. I could tell from the seriousness of his voice that the subject matter must be urgent.

Raffie smiled and calmly answered, "Well sure, son. Have a seat."

The man complied and sat down on the chair beside Raffie. I watched as he discreetly leaned in toward Raffie and said, "Sir, I know you give good advice, and everyone likes you and respects you. I have something to ask you about." His eyes furtively looked over at me.

Raffie caught the askance look toward me and said, "Don't worry—this is Paul. He is a friend."

The man looked at me, and I sensed he accepted Raffie's assurance that my presence would not breach the confidential nature of the discussion.

"Sir, my son is thirteen. His older brother got into trouble at this age. I'm afraid this son is following in his footsteps. I don't want him to get hurt or hurt someone else. I'm hearing that he's hanging around with a bad crowd of boys at school."

The old man slowly nodded, listening intently to the man's openness in discussing his fatherly situation.

The father's eyes were sad, and he spoke now in a contrite tone. "Sir, I don't know what to do. I don't want to lose him. What can I do?"

I watched the old man as he rubbed his chin in thought. He did not answer right away and instead gradually leaned toward the man in a gesture of kinship and empathy. He put his hand on the man's shoulder for a moment to comfort him. I could see that Raffie was treating the man's request with great import and gravity as he began speaking slowly. "Son, first be patient. Your son needs your love. Tell him you are proud of him and love him and he is someone special."

The man's eyes were fixed on Raffie's face, and I could see him listening intently and nodding. The father appeared to have the look that a patient has when a physician is discussing a serious health problem and what the prognosis will be.

"OK, I will try to do what you just said," he replied earnestly. "But I'm not that good at saying these things. It's not natural for me." The man looked down at the porch and said resignedly to himself, "And I know I have to do better."

"Son, try to involve him in good things he likes to do. Things that your family can experience with him. Good things your family can encourage him in. What does he like to do?"

"He mostly plays video games, hangs out after school with his friends, and listens to music." The man paused to think. "He does like baseball. He also played soccer when he was six or seven."

"Sports are good. See if he'll join a baseball league," Raffie quickly responded. "He's not too old to do that. Maybe you can help coach him in soccer. Find some simple activities you can do together. Also, if you go to church, ask him to go with you. I know that will likely be very hard. But it is best for him to separate good from bad activities in his life."

"Yes, yes, sir, I will try."

"Also, I know it can sometimes be impossible with your work schedule, but try to have dinner at home with the family each night. With everyone around the dinner table, it sends a message that he is part of a family that cares." Raffie paused and, looking at the father in his troubled state of hopelessness, tried to add encouragement. "Son, it's not hard. You just have to show him you love him. You can do this."

"I will, sir," the man answered in a more confident tone. "I know that you are right."

"Does he like to fish or hunt?" asked Raffie as he continued to think of ways to pull the son away from the bad influences in his life. "Can you take him to a sporting event? Are there things you can do together? You know, dad things."

The man's coworkers were beginning to come out through the screen door now, and they began to gather on the porch. The concerned father did not answer Raffie, and seeing his coworkers, he began to become restless and slowly stood up. I watched as the father looked down at Raffie and spoke in a quiet and sincere, appreciative tone so as not to be overheard by his coworkers. "Thank you, sir. I will try hard to do what you said. You have been very helpful."

The old man nodded calmly, not breaking the confidence this man had entrusted to him. He simply said, "Please keep me informed."

The man quietly gave a short nod of understanding and patted Raffie on the shoulder in a gesture of appreciation. He walked slowly between us toward the screen door and disappeared inside.

Raffie was now looking at the coworkers as they socialized in the parking lot. I watched them as well and thought they probably worked closely together. They bantered back and forth, and there was much laughter. I watched as a heavyset young man who was in the center said something loudly in Spanish, triggering ever more increasing laughter. I do not speak Spanish, but I could tell this young man was the center of frivolity in the group.

Raffie smiled and said blissfully, "Ah, to be young again."

*****

After most of the noon lunch crowd had departed, Raffie appeared to be in a state of semi slumber. I did not want to disturb him, and I took the liberty of standing up and stretching my legs. I also felt it was a good time to text the office and my wife, giving them updates. I pulled out my cell phone, and leaning against the railing, I quickly messaged the office and my wife about the status of my departure. I also checked my work and personal texts and emails for matters of importance. Nothing of significance required my immediate attention. I exhaled a deep sigh of relief, knowing that being stranded here was not interfering with anything noteworthy in my life as of now.

I walked to the edge of the deck, still trying to stretch my legs. It felt good to stand up for a while. The hard wooden seat and back of the chair were not very comfortable. And after a while my back was beginning to ache and stiffen up.

As midday had passed, the sun was once again casting shadows inexorably across the parking lot. At the edge of the deck, the sunlight reflecting off the windshields of parked cars was blinding, and I shielded my eyes looking across at Diego's. My car was still parked where I had left it in the morning.

Suddenly I heard a loud noise as a motorcycle shot by us along the highway. The unmuffled engine sound echoed off the porch. I could see Raffie's head jerk backward, and his startled eyes opened to survey the source of the awakening noise.

"Man, that was loud," he said, rubbing the side of his face as he gradually came out of his slumber. "You know, I used to own a motorcycle, Paul. But it didn't sound like that." He laughed to himself. "I drove it all over the country in my younger days. It was a lot of fun. Marcia would sit behind me, and we had a great time together touring rural communities. But after we had kids, I had to sell it. I'd be afraid to ride one now. Just too old."

I watched as Raffie stretched his legs out, extending his arms in the air. He looked like a half-winged bird. I could see his range of motion wasn't very good. He took his glasses off and slowly began rubbing his eyes. "Sorry if I fell asleep on you. I do take catnaps occasionally. I will pay a price for it. Probably won't sleep well tonight."

"That's quite all right," I answered. "I got a few things done I needed to do."

The old man seemed to be refreshed now and fully alert, with no lingering sleepiness. He turned to me and said, "Well, Paul, I haven't asked you an important question today. Do you like your job? Do you like what you're doing?"

I thought for a moment, pondering his question. I needed some time to think through my response, as no immediate declarative reply came to mind. But as celebrities on talk shows and in interviews often do, I began, "That's a good question." I think beginning an answer that way provides more time to think of a really good answer.

"It's a good job," I responded slowly. "The people I work with are great. The benefits are good. However, the company is very large, and there is a lot of politics I have to deal with, which is hard when I'm on the road as much as I am. The company's size makes it a bit bureaucratic and rigid at times, and it's very difficult to get things done quickly."

I could see the old man was listening intently as he took in my words, slowly nodding. After a short pause, he thoughtfully responded, "You know, Paul, as I mentioned earlier, I worked for a large national oil company when I got out of school. Similar to you, I experienced some of the pain of corporate bureaucracy. I didn't know much, and I was young and naïve. I thought I could change the company. But gradually the company changes you."

I laughed, as I could personally relate to his experience. In large organizations you change to conform to the company. If you do not conform, be prepared to be unhappy, and be prepared to accept more stress.

"Working for that petroleum company, I found out quickly," he continued, "that you can't change anything fast in a big company. Everyone is trying to keep their job or preserve their image, enhancing their prospects for future advancement. Everyone is afraid of failing and losing their position in the company. Or they are afraid of being marginalized. Decision-making is so slow because of these fears, and most decisions are not made until they are deemed safe and become no-brainers."

I nodded in agreement. What the old man said was so true.

"And Paul, that slowness in these big companies to accept new ideas and make decisions is good for the smaller, more nimble and innovative companies. You know large, bureaucratic companies are the hatcheries for small, innovative companies. After a while, employees with ambition get tired of the bureaucracy in these big companies and start their own companies from the ground up. Then the big companies buy the hatched spin-offs and turn them back into the monolithic bureaucracy." Raffie chuckled to himself. "That is American business for you. But it works."

I laughed. "It does often seem to work that way."

*****

From somewhere in the distance, in the heat of the day, I heard someone calling out my name with a Mexican accent: "Mr. Thomas. Hey, Mr. Thomas." I looked across the street and saw Diego in his blue mechanic's jumpsuit waving for me to come over.

The old man also looked up, and seeing Diego, he yelled across the highway, "Hi, Diego, how are you doing today?"

Diego yelled back, "Doing fine, Raffie. It's just too hot today. My fan doesn't work fast enough to keep me cool," he said, laughing.

I stood up and walked across the deck and went down the steps to the parking lot. As soon as I was out from under the shade of the deck, I felt the wrath of the full force of the sun. It was like stepping under a heat lamp. It felt like a warm compress had been pressed against the back of my neck. It would be hard to live in this weather, I thought.

I crossed the street and approached Diego, who was now standing in the shade in one of the automobile repair bays. He had a pleasant smile and was holding something in his hand.

As I stepped into the shade of the garage, he said, "Mr. Thomas. I got some good news. I have the part here, and I'll begin to install it. It will take a little time, though, to get it mounted and tested out. And I have a couple of cars I have to finish first. But I wanted you to know that it will be fixed today as I promised." The mechanic's face was smudged with grease. His jumpsuit clearly had many more grease spots on it than it had in the morning. As he talked to me, he maintained a constant broad and welcoming countenance. Diego just seemed like the type of person who was always in a pleasant mood.

"That's great news," I responded appreciatively.

"Yes, when it was delivered, I was happy to see it was the right part. Sometimes I've gotten parts delivered that didn't fit or were the wrong parts. But not this time."

I wanted to clarify when the repair work would be finished, as I knew getting to the airport on time would be tight. "So you still think the car will be ready by four thirty. That's still doable?"

"Oh yes, I should have the part installed and tested by then. No problem, Mr. Thomas." His eyes slowly turned away from me, and he looked now across the street at

Miggy's. "I see you have been talking to Raffie all day." As he spoke, he continued to look at the old man across the street. His expression appeared more thoughtful now, and his words slowed. "I will tell you something about Raffie. He has not been the same since his wife, Marcia, died. I've known him for a while. I've worked over the years on all his vehicles. But I never saw him much at Miggy's until after Marcia died. It hit him very hard."

Diego now turned toward me and continued, "Mr. Thomas, Raffie can talk about everything, and he's done a lot in his life. If you listen to him, he has a lot of wisdom. He's very thoughtful, and he's also an incredibly kind man."

I responded, "It seems like everybody knows him around here."

"Oh, Raffie is everybody's friend. But since he misses his wife so much, it is sad to see him just sitting there every day, usually by himself."

I was struck by how much Diego seemed to be worried about the old man. Through his eyes I could see the sincerity of his concern was deep and genuine. There was also a sadness in Diego's eyes as he continued.

"He and Marcia were very active. They traveled the world for many years. Name a place, and he's been there." Diego hesitated for a moment and began again. "And Mr. Thomas, you'd never know how well off he is by looking at him. He's a very humble man."

I looked across the street now at Raffie. He was slumped in his chair with his head down. It was really sad seeing him from this perspective, and I asked, "He sits on the porch every day?"

"Yes. Marcia died a couple of years ago, and he comes to Miggy's every day except for Sunday. I know he's got to be really lonely sitting by himself every day. It's nice that you can talk to him while you're here. I'm sure he appreciates that."

"I enjoy talking to him." I turned now to look at Diego, and I reflected on what he had just said. "You know, it's a bit funny. But just having met him today, I feel like I've known him for a while."

Diego laughed. "Everyone says that. What you may not know is he is also a very generous man to this community. He's given a lot back to this community. The city should name a park or building or something after him. But he'd object if he knew they were going to do that."

"I saw his kindness firsthand earlier on a project he believes in," I said. I looked down now at the floor of the garage. There were chips in the concrete and deep scuff marks. The bottom of each bay door was covered in spiderwebs and years of trapped insects and dust.

Diego must have seen my wandering eyes and quickly said, "OK, Mr. Thomas, I'll let you know when the car is ready. I promise it will be done before four thirty."

"Thanks. I appreciate that," I said. "Just call me across the street when it's done."

"Will do."

The old man was watching me as I returned. As I stepped up onto the deck and the respite from the sun, he said, "Diego is a good man. He can fix anything. He's the best mechanic I've ever had work on my vehicles."

"I'm not worried," I said. "He has the right part, and he promised me it will get fixed on time. I don't think I'll miss my flight home tonight."

*****

As I sat down, the old man calmly cleared his throat and began speaking slowly in a reflective and profound tone. His eyes were studying the sky as he spoke.

"Paul, as I get older, I have more time to think. I think about the world when I was younger, and I look at the world today in comparison. We've made some significant improvements, though you would not think so listening to the media nowadays."

"We are a bit polarized today," I chuckled.

"This country has changed a lot," he continued. "Sometimes for the better and sometimes for the worse. Change is not always good or great, you know, but change is not always bad or terrible. The issue is to what degree do we change, and do we change for the better?" He stopped for a moment and briefly coughed and cleared his throat again. "If I make an apple pie and I follow a recipe, I can change an ingredient here or there, but let's say I want more cinnamon or sugar than the recipe calls for. So I make that change and I bake the pie. Now when I taste the pie after changing the recipe, it might taste better, or it might taste worse. My changes may not have improved the taste of the pie. We have to be careful in this country. Change for change's sake can sometimes have negative or unintended consequences."

"There's plenty of examples of that today," I replied.

"Paul, a great tragedy can occur even when one's intentions are good—or thought to be good. We are fortunate that our founding fathers provided us a great framework, the Constitution."

"That was a monumental work for that time period. Let's hope we never get rid of it," I said, chuckling sardonically. "I don't want to lose my rights."

"Paul, if we lost the principles embedded in our Constitution, our society would suffer great harm. The Constitution gives us a framework for getting things right. In our country sometimes it does take longer to right something that is wrong, but eventually the correct action is taken. Look how much time it took for us to reverse slavery and give women the right to vote. But we have new issues today that need fixed. Some of which have been created by our politicians. But we should never ignore the principles and rights promised in the Constitution."

"That's politics," I said, shaking my head. "The government is such a leviathan."

The old man leaned forward, and the arch of his back was more pronounced now. "The good thing is that a functional democracy may be slow, but making changes in our laws, in principle, should be a steady process. Proposed changes should be studied carefully and discussed before being enacted. Democracy in action, if it is slow and thoughtful, is not always a bad thing."

Raffie sighed slowly and leaned toward me. "Paul, when I look at our issues today and compare them to the issues we had decades ago, a lot of our problems have not changed. Education, poverty, drugs, foreign wars, social division, and crime are either moving backward or have not gotten any better over the years. On the bright side, people have more freedoms of choice today, and the protective classes have more opportunities now than before. But in all our cultural transformations, we seem to have lost the concept of personal responsibility. All our problems are being cast as things caused by society. A quixotic, irrational inclination to tear down and condemn our society based on past transgressions does not solve today's problems. It only leads to more pain and distrust and resentment."

He stopped for a moment to make a point. "You know, diversity is good, but we also have to have unity with it. If we are not together, we will not be together. A civil democracy can only function so long, and will eventually fail, if its citizens refuse to take personal responsibility for their actions."

I nodded understandingly and added, "We have a lot of problems in our society today. These are really difficult times."

"Paul, they are. But there have been other moments in American history that were even more difficult compared to today. As a country we seem to have lost our focus on what is best for this country and what is in our best interest. The world couldn't care less if America is successful, and in many places in the world they would like to see us fail. And if we fail, then it will speak volumes about the limits of mankind. Our society has tried to show the rest of the world how we can have a diverse, multicultural society, live together in harmony, and still be prosperous."

This prompted me to ask, "So do you believe in American exceptionalism?"

Raffie eased back in his chair, slowly exhaling. I watched his arched back as it unrolled like an accordion on the back of the chair. "Yes, I do. Paul, I truly do. But it's not that Americans are smarter, more ambitious, or more energetic than everyone else in the world." He stopped to clear his throat again. "Sorry—when I talk too much, my throat can get dry. We are exceptional because of our economic system and economic incentives, which create great opportunities. By that I mean we have an open society where you can work hard and achieve success, and if you should fail, you can pick yourself up and try again. If a person fails, we give them second and sometimes third and fourth chances to achieve success. This economic system allows Americans to thrive. And also, because this is an ever-evolving democracy, the citizens have a right to vote for representatives to change the laws when it is necessary to do so. At least so far, we have been able to prosper without any fear of a dictatorial tyranny. But we have to work at it, to nurture it and keep it alive. Benjamin Franklin once was asked by someone, before the course of this nation was firmly established, 'Do we have a republic or a monarchy?' His answer was, 'A republic, if we can keep it.'"

Raffie stopped again to clear his throat and continued, "America reinforces itself as each generation holds on to the dream that drives self-confidence, hope, and optimism. We all move forward under the banner of the American Dream. Everyone has the potential to succeed in something they are best at. Unfortunately, not everyone can be guaranteed success. Personal decisions can and will make an impact on whether a person is successful or not. People also have different drives and different levels of self-confidence, which can affect their opportunities to be successful. But the incentives for achieving success in America are greater than in any other country, and we must never forget that. We have great opportunities in this country that in other countries are just not there. In a lot of the world, if you are born poor, you die poor. Your lot is determined by your parents or your financial and social standing at birth."

What Raffie was conveying to me made a lot of sense. The irony was that most Americans today would not speak as openly and frankly as he was doing. "Raffie, I don't think most Americans appreciate that our economic system has allowed us to achieve the standing we have in the world today. If you look at the major advances and scientific breakthroughs in the twentieth century and beyond, most have come from America."

The old man looked down at his hands now, turning them palms up as if trying to catch thoughts from above. "Our issues today, as in other times, are more political. Politics is a dirty business, and neither party has a monopoly on the truth or virtue. They think they do, but they don't. One party is accused of being mean spirited and narrow minded, and its adherents are, sometimes unjustly, broadly called racists and bigots; the other party, which touts progressiveness, is self-serving, full of elitists and hypocrites. On this last group: Look at sanctuary cities and how the citizens balk when immigrants show up on their doorstep. Look how progressives encourage antipolice movements, but when they personally are crime victims, they scream for police protection. Look at the most ardent antigun advocate who laments when someone breaks into their house that they wish they'd had a gun to protect themselves. Look at how some scream that democracy is in jeopardy, yet their actions prevent and distort democracy. And still others proclaim a desire for unity, but their actions and words destroy unity through the identity politics and cancel culture that continue to divide us. This group puts itself in an invidious position."

He stopped to clear his throat and continued, "Fascism is when the government, big business, and the media and entertainment industry are all in lockstep. I think it is these elitist groups today that are trending toward fascism. The will of the people and opposing viewpoints are suppressed by the actions of these elitists who believe they have the answer to all societal woes. Elitism is anathema to democracy. A democracy cannot function without all healthy viewpoints being equally aired and opinions freely expressed: conservative or liberal. But democracy can only work with some level of compromise. And to that point, we should work in a civil manner to reach compromises that are in the best interest of this country.

But we should never compromise on the truth. Politicians miss this point often and try to cloud the truth or make up their own truths to fit their narratives. But the truth is the truth."

Raffie stopped and chuckled to himself. "I hate to point out one group in this country that is at the pinnacle of hypocrisy. But we have the entertainment industry. Real people in a make-believe world whose most vocal members today are mostly elitist." His chuckle now grew into a pronounced laugh of disbelief. "Only in Hollywood can a five-foot-six, one-hundred-twenty-pound woman beat up five two-hundred-pound muscular men simultaneously. Is that entertainment or aspirational propaganda? Paul, today the entertainment industry is more aspirational than inspirational. It should be the other way around."

The old man stopped, and turning, he looked at me eye to eye. "So which is worse, the party that is more realistic and merit oriented and slow to change, or the party that is too idealistic, elitist, and hypocritical?"

I smiled. "I can't answer that question. Both have flaws."

"Exactly. Political groups espousing either excessive idealism or excessive realism can be destructive to a democracy and our individual freedoms. This is where civil compromise has to occur, or we will quit being a democracy."

I nodded, understanding his concerns about the deleterious impact on society from the polarization of politics.

"And today we sometimes mix social issues wrongly with economic issues." The old man's eyes grew wider, but his voice remained modulated. "Have you heard of Milton Friedman?"

I took economics in college, and we studied Friedman's economic theories. "Yes, I know he was an economist," I responded.

"Paul, you know Friedman was quite an intelligent man. I would think he would be troubled by our societal economic approaches today. It seems like some people believe that all outcomes should be equal, regardless of one's abilities or work efforts. Friedman had a famous quote on the distribution of wealth: 'A society that puts equality before freedom will get neither. A society that puts freedom before equality will get a high degree of both.' The idealistic beliefs of pushing income equality and equity regardless of one's ability and work ethic eventually will erode our personal freedoms. Democracy only truly works when it encourages and rewards efforts to be in harmony. If it does not, there is a fine line between pushing and enforcing unfair practices and an authoritarian police state."

*****

As I sat there thinking about what he had said, a small red foreign sedan pulled into the parking lot and stopped in front of the porch. I watched as a middle-aged woman and a teenager got out from each side of the car. The woman wore a colorful blouse and white shorts. The teenager had a T-shirt on over a pair of dark jeans. Raffie looked up and immediately recognized the approaching pair. He greeted them, saying, "Well, hello, how are you doing, Maria?"

The middle-aged woman smiled and responded, "Fine, Mr. Raffie. But it's too hot."

The old man laughed. "It's July—what would you expect? I see you brought your daughter."

The mother and daughter stepped up onto the deck, and the daughter smiled at the both of us and then looked down at the floor of the deck in a bashful way. She stood quietly by her mother's side. I could see she was rather unsettled and uncomfortable in this social environment with older adults.

"Carmen," said the mother. "Come over here and sit beside Mr. Raffie."

The daughter still did not look up, but she slowly walked over to the chair beside the old man and sat down.

The mother began speaking. "Mr. Raffie, you may not know this, but Carmen received one of your college scholarships. She has done really well in her studies at the high school."

Raffie turned to the daughter and smiled. "I did not know that, but congratulations on receiving the scholarship. You must be pretty smart."

A slight smile appeared on the teenager's face. Then she softly said, "Thank you for the scholarship, Mr. Raffie. I have applied to get into a big school. But I'm not sure what I want to do."

The mother quickly added, "Mr. Raffie, we thought you might be able to help Carmen. Maybe you could make some suggestions. What would you say she should study in college?"

The old man leaned back in his chair and looked at the mother and then the daughter. He was slow to speak and spoke in a measured voice: "Well, I can't make that decision for you. Carmen, what do you want to do? And what subjects have you done well in at the high school?"

Carmen looked at her mother as if looking for approbation to speak. The mother nodded, and then the young girl turned to Raffie and began, "I would like to be an engineer. I'm good at math and science. I think I could be a good engineer." She stopped and looked back at her mother again and then continued slowly, "But some people think I would not do well as an engineer."

The old man paused for a moment, taking in the timid daughter's words, and then said, "Why do some people think you will not do well?"

The mother interjected, looking at Raffie. "Well, girls usually don't do engineering. You don't see very many women engineers."

The old man turned to the daughter now and spoke to her in a sincere, caring tone. "Carmen, as I said, I cannot tell you what to study in college. But if you want to be an engineer, you should study to be an engineer. It is important that whatever you decide to study is something you really want to do. Do not let others talk you out of what you want to do. You studied hard in high school and did well—you can do likewise in college. Being an engineer is a good job, and you can make a good living at it."

The mother spoke up again. "She's also afraid that she might end up like her cousins."

Raffie asked, "Why is she concerned about being like her cousins? What happened to them?"

The mother responded, "Well, they went to college by borrowing a lot of money. They got big student loans. But the degrees they graduated with are worthless, and they can't find jobs. They now have large student loan payments each month and have only a little income to make their payments."

The old man sighed and looked at me and the mother. "The full scholarship should prevent that from happening to Carmen. But in regard to her cousins and all these kids with huge student loans with little or no means to pay them back, I blame that problem on the universities and our federal government. They've turned the universities into businesses that grow on government support. The students get run through an academic treadmill, and if they borrow to attend college, they graduate with a huge amount of debt and degrees that sometimes are in fields with very limited potential income."

The mother added, "We also have a second cousin who graduated with a degree in retail business administration, and after five years he is now an apprentice plumber. But he is doing well and can make his student loan payments."

The old man sighed again. "Unfortunately these young kids today are being pushed into going to college. Our society is telling them there are no opportunities for non-college graduates. But that is not true. We are just sending too many kids to college these days, and often they would be better off financially not going to college. They should be getting into the trades, like plumbing or being electricians or working up through an organization that pays for their education."

I could see that Raffie had become energized by the topic of this conversation. I even sensed that it was like caffeine to his soul. His voice was sharper now, and his eyes brightened as he expressed his thoughts and feelings toward this disservice to some of the youth in America.

"Carmen, I can only tell you to pursue your dreams. The biggest regret you could have in your life is not doing that. Don't let anyone talk you out of it. No one should make that decision for you. If you make the decision yourself, you and only you will know if it is the right decision."

The daughter nodded appreciatively and appeared to be momentarily relieved from the stress that had built up regarding her future plans. She smiled more freely now and seemed more at ease. I think she was glad about what the old man had told her. The mother nodded as well and seemed also to be satisfied with Raffie's advice. I thought maybe they felt that this onerous burden of uncertainty had been lifted from their lives and was behind them now. And maybe that a clear path was ahead of them, and they could proceed with greater certainty and confidence.

The mother came over to Raffie and, with a broad smile, reached out and shook his hand. "Mr. Raffie, I want to thank you for everything you have done to help our daughter. Her father and I couldn't afford to send her to the schools she is applying to. You are such a thoughtful and generous person. God bless you."

Raffie looked over at me and seemed rather embarrassed by the sudden outflowing of appreciation. "You're welcome," he said, looking down at the floor, and then he looked up at Carmen. "But you did it. I just provided some assistance. Keep that in mind, Carmen—you earned the scholarship. But I do have just one favor to ask."

The daughter looked up and smiled apprehensively, asking, "Mr. Raffie, what is that?"

"If I'm still living and able to attend, I want to be invited to your engineering graduation party," he said, laughing, with a broad, extended smile.

The mother and daughter laughed as well and simultaneously responded, "You will be invited, Mr. Raffie. Trust us."

After the mother and daughter had left, the old man turned to me and said, "It's sad to say this. Some of our universities are in trouble today. They are run by the elitist class structure. My wish is that Carmen will not be forced to conform to their world. In some of these institutions of higher learning, there are individuals who profess open-mindedness to the point of being closed minded. They cloak themselves in intellectual malarky and groupthink. They can speak using big words and confusing language, all the while arrogantly believing their viewpoint is so altruistic, pure, and virtuous that it cannot be challenged. They believe that life and our society can only be shaped one way—their way. And that dissenters and dissidents are cretins, either wrong minded or unintelligent." Raffie stopped and coughed again, clearing his throat. "Should they be considered the arbiters of Carmen's life and our lives?"

"I would hope not," I answered, thinking about how when I was in college we were told to think independently and be open to new ideas, and simultaneously not to condemn any reasonable alternate viewpoint. It is quite amazing how the concept of reason and logic and open-mindedness on some college campuses has changed over the last twenty-five years.

*****

A few minutes later, an old blue Ford F-150 pickup truck pulled up covered in dust, with numerous dents and several scratches on the hood. The side doors opened, and several men climbed out and proceeded to walk toward us. Raffie looked up, and I could tell he did not recognize any of the men. They were wearing faded construction clothes, and each had his own unique ball cap. One of the men had his shirt off, displaying an evenly coated tan. They passed with a casual "Good afternoon" and walked inside Miggy's. About ten minutes later, the men walked out, drinking from large white Styrofoam cups and carrying bags of chips and wrapped sandwiches. They cajoled each other, laughing, and two of them casually began pushing each other, jockeying for who would sit in the front seat of the truck. One of the men who had walked past us toward the truck suddenly turned around as if he had forgotten something. He looked up at us and with a cavalier flair smiled, saying, "Have a good day, gentlemen."

Raffie watched them intently as they all climbed into the truck, still laughing and harassing each other in playful frivolity. I thought that, like others that day, they seemed like a happy bunch and probably worked well together as a team. Once they pulled away, Raffie turned to me and said, "Those men are the salt of the earth. When America loses the trust of those men, we will cease being a great country. It is men and women like that that keep America running. I am not belittling anyone who is working in an office. But for everyone sitting in an office working a white-collar job, there are thousands of people working in the trades and in the fields. And they are just as important and necessary to keep everything going. And these people are smart in many different ways. Think about it—look at someone in the construction business. Each day they are confronted with unique problems while constructing a building. Each structure is different, and they have to apply their knowledge and skills to complete their tasks. They have to be able to read and follow blueprints, and if something is unique, they have to be creative and find work-arounds. That knowledge comes from their personal experience and from discussing with others in the trade to find solutions, and it's not all school taught."

The old man looked at me now, squinting over his thick eyebrows. "I've worked with rig workers in the hottest part of Texas and some of the coldest parts of Alaska, and I've worked with high-powered bankers, merger-and-acquisition investment people, and big-city lawyers." He paused for a moment and chuckled slowly. "The guys in the field I trusted a lot more. They knew how to appreciate what they had and were not hung up on social standing, self, and wealth."

Hearing Raffie's words, I realized I had just been placed in his untrustworthy group, since I was a banker—the group he identified as being hung up on social standing, self, and wealth. I felt a little self-conscious about that and slyly smiled. "Well, I'm a banker, Raffie. I guess I'm in the group you don't trust as much."

Raffie turned toward me, shaking his head, and said, "Not you, Paul. You're different. I think you get it. Not everyone understands our country today," he continued. "The elitists continually push a top-down approach to corral and string everyone together like paper cutouts. But in America we are different from other countries in that we have fifty separate states with fifty different places to exercise our freedom. It gives each of us a wide latitude to select where we wish to enjoy the most salient rights that we personally cherish the most."

I had not thought of our country that way, but it begged a question, and I said, "That's true, but our federal government makes the overriding laws we are all subject to as a nation. States can't run the military or interstate commerce."

The old man nodded in agreement and continued, "Yes, the federal government has to manage certain elements of our society. But personal choices must exist in a true democracy, and that's why we need fifty state governments. For instance, if education is important to you or for your children, you can move to a state with better schools. If you don't want to be taxed excessively, you can move to a lower-tax state. If you are concerned about needing a later-term abortion, for example, you can either move to a state offering that option or have the procedure done in a state that gives you that option. If crime is an issue, then move to a state or city with stricter enforcement laws. If you want more social welfare payments, move to a state that offers more publicly funded subsistence programs. Gun laws and parental rights are different in different states, and some states are more business friendly. This is unlike most every other country in the world. That's why we are the United States, and we still have state rights. We must never lose those rights. Not all strong central governments are tyrannical, but all tyrannical governments are fully centralized."

As I pondered Raffie's words, I looked out at the simmering asphalt highway. A large tractor trailer roared by at that moment, kicking up a cloud of dust. All morning trucks had passed by, kicking up wave after wave of dust. As each huge eighteen-wheeler flew by us, it made a thunderous sound that shook the floor of the deck. As the trucks passed, the fading sound would trail off down the road. I was thinking to myself that Raffie was providing me a good lesson on civics. He seemed to be steeped in common sense, and I did not feel that he was lecturing to me or being didactic, but just that he was conveying his perspectives on America. In a time where absolute truths are bent and dismissed, and when something that is absolutely right can be construed as being wrong, his approach was refreshing. And at a time where rational, populist opinions are not usually expressed in public, I found myself agreeing with much of what he was saying. I could tell he had given much thought to his words. I was also impressed with his diverse knowledge and ability to think deeply. He had a calculating, logical mind and seemed to understand the sources of problems and be able to identify easier approaches to fixing them. I think people that are, or were, in positions that require problem-solving skills, as Raffie had been in owning his own company, get very frustrated when problems get kicked like a can down the road. They believe in solving real problems before they become bigger issues. I think some people are just better equipped to solve problems, and then others are better at just soldiering on. And then others just throw their hands up in the air and give up. I always believed I was in one of the first two categories.

*****

I was becoming ever more intrigued by Raffie, and I really wanted to hear more about his life. What made him tick? Why did he so deeply care about America's future? Had he ever thought he was going to fail in life? How had he overcome the difficulties in his life? I did not know the answers to these questions, but I did know that his answers would come with wisdom, without any tone of bitterness, rancor, or regret. There was a calming effect in his voice that made him very likeable. He spoke with certainty, but he was not domineering or overbearing. There was a positive karma about him. I had never met anyone quite like him, and he had pulled me into the vortex of his world with great affinity.

I began by asking him what I thought was rather a frivolous question. "I understand you've traveled a lot. Diego mentioned it to me. Where would you recommend taking a family on a vacation?"

Raffie thought for a minute. I could sense he was formulating an answer. "First, I'm glad you are including your kids in your vacations. Whenever possible, Marcia and I took our kids with us when we traveled. Even when we went overseas. It is a good thing for children to see other cultures and places in the world. And I might add, there are many places in America they should see also." He stopped, seemingly waiting again to think how to answer my question thoroughly. Then he continued speaking slowly: "I would recommend first visiting the major capitals of Europe. London, Paris, Rome, Madrid, and Athens. In Paris you must see Versailles, and in Rome you must see the Vatican. I'd also recommend taking a river cruise down the Danube and Rhine. Preferably in the early fall or late springtime. Germany, Austria, and France have beautiful countrysides. It's a long way away, but the sounds in New Zealand are spectacular. Japan is another great visit and also exposes your children to a completely different culture. You should at least once in your lifetime take a safari in Africa. It's something to see the animals in the wild and meet the local people. Rio is an exciting place, and I personally like Buenos Aires. And of course, there are many other places, but that is enough to get you started. Have you been to any of the places I've mentioned?"

"A few. I've been to London and Paris. We did vacation with the kids in Italy last year and were in Rome."

We had gone to London and Paris before we had children and had visited Italy with our children the previous summer. Italy was an enjoyable trip, and I think our kids got as much out of it as we did. The northern Italian countryside was a beautiful experience.

"Paul, I must admit that since I can speak Spanish and English, I'm a bit partial to places where I have no problems communicating. But you don't have to go far to experience great travel adventures. There are great places in the United States to visit as well. It's nice to see different parts of our country and yet feel like you are at home." He stopped to clear his throat for a moment and continued, "I'm sure you've done some traveling in our country. There are plenty of educational things for your kids in New York City and Washington DC. It's also enjoyable to visit San Diego and Denver and, though it's been fading of late, San Francisco. I also like Miami—it's a great cosmopolitan city. Orlando is a great city for the family. San Antonio's River Walk at night is something to see. And a surprising city to visit is Kansas City if you stay downtown. They have the only World War I museum in the country." He added as an afterthought, "Some other places you should visit at least once in your lifetime, unless you already have been there, are New Orleans and Las Vegas." He quietly laughed to himself. "But don't bring the kids."

I had been to many of the places he had mentioned and had enjoyed the visits, some with family and some strictly on business. I agreed with Raffie that when we traveled domestically, everything was easier and much more predictable. Being able to speak the local language made it all more pleasant.

The old man had indeed visited many places, and I could tell he liked to travel and encourage others to do so as well. I thought he probably missed that aspect of his life since he was older now and alone.

"Paul, America is a beautiful country. There are states where you can be in the cool mountains in the morning and on a sunny, warm beach in the afternoon. I've settled down here in this arid climate, but I think those who can afford to live year-round in moderate weather have it the best."

I thought about his last statement and curiously inquired, "If I may ask, what brought you to live here?"

Raffie leaned back in his chair, straightening his back as much as he could. "I don't practice what I preach when I say where it is best to live. I live here because this place was special to my wife. Marcia liked living here. She had family just south of here, on the other side of the border. We would visit them occasionally, and I would help her family financially from time to time. I believe in providing for people and family who really are in need. You know, people not just looking for a handout but a hand up, if you know what I mean?" I nodded, understanding his point. Raffie paused again, and I could see a look of concern invade his countenance. "It's tough down there south of the border, and most of the folks are good, hardworking people. But they have some bad people and corrupt politicians. In America we tend to trust our government and institutions. Down there it is not always that way. If our country should ever change and allow government officials, the justice system, the military, and the media to be corrupted and controlled by the wrong people, I am afraid we would be just like them. It's the human nature to excessively control others that drives bad government actions."

"I've heard some horror stories about Americans traveling down there. Did you ever encounter any problems traveling south of the border?" I asked.

"No, nothing that comes to mind, but it is dangerous down there in certain parts of the countryside," he responded. "I won't go down there anymore at my age. Well, maybe other than the well-protected tourist areas. I am an old man, and I could be robbed and held for ransom or just disappear. The environment is different there, and you do not always trust the police or the military to do the right thing." He turned to me, and I could see his piercing dark eyes looking straight into mine. "Paul, I will tell you a story about what happened to me about twenty years ago on one of my visits. I had to be airlifted from Chihuahua to a hospital in

Albuquerque. I had eaten at a restaurant that had tainted pork, and I got really sick. They rushed me to the hospital that night in Chihuahua. I have to say they had great doctors and nurses, and they did the best they could for me. But my situation got worse, as I was diagnosed with gastroenteritis and an intestinal infection. There was a moment when I thought I was going to die there. I lost ten pounds in the first two days." He stopped, and the tenor of his voice changed. He looked down at the floor of the deck and started to speak in a warm, melancholy tone. "My love, Marcia, arranged a charter medical helicopter from Albuquerque to pick me up. She saved my life."

I was watching his face as he spoke. I could see that the memory of this event had triggered the grieving of the loss of his wife again. I thought that at his age maybe that feeling would never go completely away from him. I thought that as he clung on to these more tender memories of her, it only strengthened his love for her.

"That must have been very tough on the both of you," I said, and then I asked, "How long did it take you to recover when you got back to the States?"

The old man studied the deck beneath his feet as he recalled his ordeal. "I was in the hospital for five weeks, getting pumped full of antibiotics and other medicines to treat the gastroenteritis and infections. They had an IV in me the whole time. The doctors and nurses were great and took good care of me. Eventually I made a full recovery, with no further problems that I'm aware of, thank God." He smiled wryly to himself and continued, "The nurses knew I was well when they couldn't stop me from talking. You may not believe this, but sometimes I can talk too much. And I can get quite ornery when I'm not feeling well. But Paul, Marcia was not going to let me die in Chihuahua."

I could tell that Raffie was very appreciative of the folks who had worked to save his life. Listening to him recall the experience, I also understood again the deep appreciation he had for his wife and how she must have loved him so much. He continued slowly, "You know, Paul, I still stay in contact with the doctors and nurses from that hospital. Whenever I'm in Albuquerque, I take all of them, even the ones who now are retired, out to dinner. I ask them to invite their spouses, and we have a great time at wherever they wish to dine."

"I bet they like it when you come to town," I said. "It sounds like it's an enjoyable evening."

"Nothing more enjoyable than still living," he responded quickly.

The early-afternoon shadows continued lengthening across the parking lot, and the traffic on the highway was now mostly semitrucks and short-carry delivery trucks. The sun was still relentless, and the arid air seared through me like a knife.

*****

The old man reclined into the chair, and as he looked into the distance, he said, "Paul, I was the sixth child of nine kids in our family. Four girls and five boys. To say we were poor is an understatement. I grew up in South Texas, and my mom and dad worked so hard to keep our family fed and clothed. My dad really had so little time to spend with us. He was always at a job—sometimes he was working three or more jobs, and he would come home late in the evening completely exhausted."

I sat listening intently to each word from the old man as he began speaking freely about his family and childhood. I was going to remain quiet, and I was not going to interrupt him. I had to know his story and wanted to hear more.

"My dad truly loved my mother," he continued. "My dad truly loved me also. But we didn't have the father-son relationship that many sons have. He just wasn't home very often. He showed his love to each of us the only way he could: by providing for us. He died my second year in college. I came home for the funeral. He worked so hard. When I think back now, I realize he probably worked himself to death just to support my mother and our family."

"My mother, she was so good to us." He paused and gazed up into the sky. I could sense a real fondness he felt toward his mother. "She worked equally hard trying to keep us fed and doing the right things. She took us to the cathedral every service, and she was a devout believer. My parents couldn't provide everything we wanted. But they did the best they could. The best was just providing us a good family life."

"Paul, as I said, we were dirt poor, and we survived only on hard work and some help from the local community around us. But even though we didn't have any money, we were happy. Growing up, I had a lot of fun with my brothers and sisters. You don't need to be rich to be happy."

He stopped to scratch the side of his neck. "The first time I ever wore new clothes was when I was given my military fatigues and dress uniform. Having something brand new to wear was an unexpected pleasure. Paul, I was honored to wear that new dress uniform. The sleeves and pants were perfectly pressed, and I was so proud of it. I was also proud of what it stood for and that I was committed to serving and protecting our country. I wore my pressed uniform in town when I was home on leave. I always got a lot of encouraging comments from the old men and women in town."

I smiled at Raffie as he recollected the feeling of pride he had felt in wearing a new pressed service uniform. I imagined that for someone who had grown up so poor and lived without so many things, that simple pleasure meant so much to him.

"But Paul, my family also experienced a lot of hardship and sadness. My brother who was just two years older than me drowned in a pond down the street from our house. I was just eight years old. It was a sad time for our family." I could see that it was still difficult for Raffie to talk about what had happened to his brother. "I wonder what Alexandro would be like today," he continued. "He was smarter and more athletic than me. As I grow older, I think about things like that. As a kid sometimes you idolize your older brothers and sisters. I can still see him in my mind wearing a T-shirt and cutoff jeans and no shoes. We all dressed like that to stay cool in the heat."

*****

Suddenly, I heard a cell phone ringing, and Raffie, with much difficulty, reached into the front pocket of his worn pants and pulled out a cell phone. He looked at the caller identification on the screen and then slowly raised it to his ear. Before speaking into the phone, he turned to me and said, "Excuse me, Paul. I have to take this call. It's business."

"Hi, Meghan," he began. "I thought you might call me today. How are you doing?"

I could see he was listening intently to the caller. He had a serious look on his face. He said "Hmmm" a few times and smiled occasionally but didn't begin speaking into the phone again for some time until he finally said, "OK, I understand. I'm sitting here outside Miggy's, on the front porch." The person on the phone spoke again, and Raffie laughed and amusedly said, "As always, I know."

I watched as the old man's face slightly relaxed, and he spoke with an exactness that belied his normal casual, informal style of conversation. He was now speaking in a businesslike tone. "Well, that all makes sense, Meghan. Prices are up for commercial properties in that market. I agree it's a good time to sell the building in Tucson. There is definitely a demand for it, and it's in a great location. One of a kind. But shouldn't we counteroffer the buyer for a little more? I know we have a big long-term capital gain, but I think we could get at least ten percent more. Don't you think so?"

The caller on the phone spoke again. Raffie listened with a pleasant smile on his face and answered, "Perfect, Meghan. Let me know what the buyer says. Also, any movement on the property in Dallas? What about the three lots in Miami we discussed the other day?" He listened intently to the caller again and responded, "Great, Meghan. It indeed has been a good year so far. How's your mother doing? Is she recovering OK?"

He listened again to the caller. "That's great. I'm glad to hear that. Tell her I was praying for her. And Meghan, as always, I appreciate everything you are doing for me.

Thanks so much. I'll see you in October, I guess. You have a nice day. Keep me posted." I watched as Raffie put the cell phone down to his side and pushed it back into his frayed pants pocket.

He looked at me and said apologetically, "Sorry, Paul. I'm retired, but sometimes you'd never know it. There still are things I have to do and take care of. I never took up golf, so business is my hobby, I suppose."

I looked at the old man, admiring how he could move freely from a personal, affable conversation into a serious business discussion without skipping a beat. I thought this was probably one of the reasons he had been able to do so well in the business world. His story was one of success and overcoming the hardships of life. He was born without much to begin with other than the love and dedication of his family. But through his hard work and being keen to opportunities, he had done well. I could tell he was a shrewd businessman who left nothing on the table. But at the same time, he was kind and generous, and he believed in giving back to others who were less fortunate. I was thinking to myself that this old man was truly a good and just man.

As I sat there taking in the old man's family story, I wondered about the rest of his family. I asked him, "How are your brothers and sisters doing? What do they do for a living?"

Raffie turned toward me and responded, "Paul, my oldest brother was a laborer and passed away a couple of years ago. He was a good Christian man who fought his lung cancer for many years. He was a heavy smoker. My oldest sister is retired after working in a hospital in Waco for many years. She has three children who all live near her now. My second-oldest sister is very quiet and was a waitress for most of her life until she opened her own restaurant. She's now turned it over to her children to run. She's very kind and gives a lot back to the community. I have two brothers younger than me, and their paths went in opposite directions. My youngest brother can't stay out of trouble and has a bit of a drinking problem that has put him in jail several times. My other brother owns a franchise shoe store in a big mall in San Antonio. He's done really well, and he can sell anything. My other two sisters are retired after years of working in retail. Paul, we are a close family and talk to one another a lot. I have tried to help all of them, giving them seed money to start businesses or helping to pay their living expenses and for their kids' education." He paused, and I sensed he was reflecting for a moment on his family. "You know, even within a family there is diversity. We all are different. We have different personalities, different things make each of us happy, and each of us is motivated in different ways."

I started thinking about my sister and brother and thought how the old man's words rang true with my family. Each of us had a separate and different life, and sometimes you would never know we were raised in the same family.

*****

A faded blue pickup truck slowly pulled off the road and coasted to a stop in front of the grocery. The pickup truck's windshield and hood were covered in a thick patina of dust, and I wondered how the driver saw through the windshield to drive. Gradually the driver's side door opened, swinging out arduously as if the occupant was struggling to exit the vehicle. The truck door made an eerily creaking sound like it had not been opened for some time. I watched as a scuffed brown boot appeared from behind the truck door, stamping the ground and causing a puff of dust to emanate in the air. Then the other boot hit the ground, and I could see that the driver was an older man. He was wearing a long sleeved shirt with both sleeves folded up to his elbows. He also wore a pair of discolored blue jeans that extended over the tops of his worn boots. The most striking feature that adorned this gentleman was a straw cowboy hat with the side brims curled up, touching the crown of the hat. As he started to walk toward the porch, I observed he had a noticeable limp. I thought to myself, this truly is a cowboy. He could have played any part in any western movie ever made. And as he got closer to the porch, I had to squint due to the sunlight reflecting off his large metallic belt buckle. Raffie was resting now and did not see the man approaching.

"Howdy, gentlemen," the old man said in a deep, raspy voice as he gazed from me to Raffie. I immediately thought that his gravelly voice matched perfectly with his countenance and cowboy attire.

Raffie suddenly looked up. "Well, well, look what the tumbleweed rolled in. How are you doing, Sergeant Manny?"

"As well as can be expected for an old man."

I watched as the old cowboy laboriously took one step at a time until he reached the base of the steps. He then firmly grabbed the stair rail with his right hand and hoisted himself up one step at a time. With each pull and step up he made a slight grunt, evidencing the effort.

Once he had firmly planted his feet on the deck, he pointed a long-bent finger toward me. "Who is this young fella here?"

Raffie smiled, and before I could answer he said, "He's a friend. Paul's his name. He's here for the day while Diego fixes his car."

The old cowboy looked at me again, and I could see clearly his weathered face under the shade of the porch.

"Diego is a great mechanic. He'll get your car running again. But Paul, you have to hang out with better people in this town."

Raffie chuckled. "Thank you, Manny, you old geezer." The old cowboy chuckled to himself, breaking into a cough. "What do you have to say today, gentlemen?"

Raffie spoke up, smiling. "We are going to try to fix everything wrong with our country."

I laughed at Raffie's response and the old cowboy turned to me and said, "Well, Paul, you'll need more than one day here."

Raffie and I chuckled amusedly. Raffie asked, "Manny, how's your back doing today? Are you getting any medical help for it?"

"I'm waiting for the VA clinic to get me a surgery date. I've been waiting three months now. I need to call them again tomorrow."

"If I can help you, let me know, Manny. I know some folks down there."

The old cowboy shook his head. "I'm fine. I don't need no help. Thanks anyway." Then the old cowboy said, "Well, gentlemen, please excuse me, but I got to get my shopping done for the week."

I watched as he opened the screen door and disappeared inside. The porch was quiet now, and in the heat of the day Raffie quickly nodded off, his lower jaw resting against his chest. As I watched the vehicles pass by the store, not focusing on anything in particular, Raffie suddenly awoke and seemed compelled to tell me more about his life. "Paul, I have to say the most difficult time in my life was when I was in the military in Vietnam. I was an eighteen-year-old in a strange country with danger always around me. I was scared to death at times, and the only comfort was that as an infantryman you always have a comradery within your platoon. I was also comforted firmly in my faith, which helped me to get through that difficult time." He coughed to clear his throat. "Military life is a sacrifice that you make—and your family makes, if you're married. The military can teach you skills and discipline, but it extracts a firm one hundred percent commitment of your life. I have to say the military did me good. It helped pay for my education and taught me about discipline and how to be committed to a purpose. It also taught me to pay attention to details and setting objectives. Which is so important in the business world, as you know."

He stopped for a moment to scratch his arm and shoulder and then continued reflecting on his life. "I think a lot of young people today could benefit from military service. You know, as a young boy staring up at the starry night sky over the prairie, I would never have imagined doing anything but following my dad in working odd jobs to make a living every day. And I'm sure I would have done well and ultimately been equally happy. But the military changed my life. It set me on a difficult course. It reset my life."

Raffie stopped for a moment, and the tone of his voice gradually became more somber as he reminisced. "You know, it was hard coming back stateside during the war. What made my experience worse was the unpopularity of the war. When I came back, many of the people I met in college didn't like the fact that I had been in the military. The students around me thought I had sold out and should have resisted the war. I was older than most of them, which was a bit strange. But I stayed friendly with all of them, even though I didn't agree with their opinions about the war and the military. We would all go to parties together and to the movies, and we talked a lot about everything. I just tried to avoid, whenever possible, talking about the war."

Raffie leaned back in his chair and turned to me to make a point. "I think today we have a problem in that young people, and sometimes older people, don't know how to disagree. If you take a stand on something socially or politically and a person disagrees with you today, it seems that either you are cancelled or blackballed or efforts are made to discredit you or ruin your reputation."

"Cancel culture I guess didn't exist in the sixties," I said, smiling.

He chuckled slowly. "No, it did. But it wasn't as bad as today. We need to open the conversation up today. We need contrasting viewpoints and ideas to be expressed freely. As I said before, no political party or viewpoint has a total monopoly on virtue or truth. We need to listen today to all reasonable viewpoints. And if I am not persuaded to change, which most of the time happens, I should agree calmly to disagree and move on." The old man paused again. "As I said before, the real truth should never be debatable. The truth is colorless, genderless, and cultureless. Again, there are many people today that believe their viewpoint is the only correct viewpoint. They are closed-minded. They think that if you don't understand their viewpoint, it's because you're not intelligent enough to understand or you are some type of crazy extremist. When these narrow-minded individuals are confronted with the real truth, they usually explode and respond by raising their voices and ignoring the other viewpoint. They often don't defend their viewpoint but attack your viewpoint. It becomes a contest as to who can speak louder and faster. They want free speech—as long as your counter viewpoint is not spoken in public. And they know that if the counter viewpoint is not known by the public, it cannot be an acceptable option."

Raffie coughed and cleared his throat. "You know my feelings on the current elite class structure in America.

They want to control everyone and everything. They usually are quite comfortable in life and feel compelled to support a social cause that I don't have any problem with, as long as they truly support that cause. Some are very naive and don't seem to understand human nature and politics. Sometimes they lack common sense. Many misinterpret and bend and modify history to suit their narrative. But some simply are self-serving. They take the path of least resistance and the path that mostly benefits them in their hope of getting better acclaim and acceptance. Paul, I have to believe there may be a small few of the elitists, but not many, who are truly genuine, and their words are consistent with their actions."

"You're probably right—there aren't very many," I said. I couldn't think of anyone off the top of my head. The only ones I could think of were the really virtuous people who personally got involved in helping others. I wouldn't call them elitist, but people like Mother Teresa, Jimmy Carter, or Albert Schweitzer. But then I thought that there are thousands of anonymous volunteers who are not elitist and work helping others every day in their communities who do not expect anything in return. They will receive no fame or glory, and yet they work tirelessly helping others in need.

The old man sighed to himself and scooted forward in his chair. I sensed he was getting uncomfortable sitting in the hard wooden chair. "Paul, we live in a free country, and I think it is totally acceptable and good to take stands against injustices. But I personally would like to see the elitists put more of their money where their mouths are. If they wish to address homelessness, racial disparity, and other social needs and causes, they should also give a considerable amount of their wealth to address these issues. I'm not talking about investing in political parties and candidates either. That can lead to election interference or promoting and supporting a party's propaganda. I want to see them donate a significant portion of their net worth to help humanity and the causes they support."

The afternoon sun beat down on the dusty parking lot. The heat was still building, and I could feel my throat drying out in this arid world. I saw a small bird racing across the road and around the back of Diego's garage. It was mostly brown and had a light, feathery belly. The bird's head had a noticeable crest. I thought that only the most rugged animals could survive in this environment. And I knew most of the dangerous ones came out at night.

"Did you see that roadrunner?" Raffie asked. "That asphalt had to be hot on his feet."

"I did," I answered. "I had never seen one before."

"I don't think any ole coyote is going to catch that one," Raffie said, laughing.

I watched as the old man yawned, and then he turned to me and continued, "Paul, I believe in this country, and I want a strong America. But at times our federal government can create more problems while trying to fix problems. Their solutions to problems are often counterproductive. Look how welfare and housing and benefit programs have ruined the family structure in some of our lower economic classes. Look how the education in this country has suffered under federal government mismanagement. Look how crime and homelessness and mental illness still remain as problems, even with more government spending. The more our government spends on health care, the more it costs us. And Paul, don't get me wrong—I'm not blaming any one party or politician."

"I guess we need better people in government," I said. Then, thinking about what he had just said, I asked, "So you don't have any faith at all in our government and in the politicians to solve our problems?"

"Paul, I have faith in good people. People that work for the good of the people and the good of our nation. People that can execute on the best ideas and solutions derived from an open society where public debate is civil and all viewpoints are heard. A totally inclusive society where people with different viewpoints are heard and respected." He stopped, and with a slight chuckle he added, "But no, I do not have faith in most of our politicians today. Especially those that couch everything in rhetoric, ignore real truths, and ignore the will of the people. And as I have said, I don't have a lot of faith either in the elitists running universities or businesses or the entertainment industry—the people who try to influence the politicians with their giving to campaigns to achieve their own interests. And I'm sad to say this, but I don't have much faith in most of the news organizations today either. These folks often filter and distort the truth and conceal opposing viewpoints. Some are even condescending in their ways, as if they are the sole keepers and purveyors of knowledge, and they will only emit what they want you to believe. They don't trust that you and I can discern the truth and act responsibly with the truth. In the end, they often end up pushing a party's propaganda with blinders on."

The old man paused, looking out over the street now, and added, "The parties today seem to want to place a nomenclature on everything to either vilify or soften a citizen's viewpoint on people and issues. In the past, everyone who was liberal was classified as communist, un-American, or socialist. That was wrong. However, there were indeed some true communists in the entertainment industry and the federal government before the true evils of communism were discovered midcentury. Today we throw the terms 'Nazi' and 'fascist' around in referring to people on the right, diluting the true nature of these evils. Paul, have you ever read the book *The Rise and Fall of the Third Reich?*"

"No, I have not. I have heard of it."

"Well, read that book. And then look around and tell me who today in the political world is a Nazi or fascist, as those terms are used to discredit individuals today in our society." Raffie looked at me, shaking his head to dismiss such nonsense. "As I said earlier, I would contend that the collusion between big government, big business, universities, the mainstream media, and the entertainment industry today is more akin to fascism. This is why we need to balance the public discourse again to include all viewpoints, except those that disrespect segments of our society and individuals. The concentration of power within a single party viewpoint is anathema to democracy. We need a press that challenges government officials regardless of their political party or viewpoint. Suppressing voices will only make those voices stronger and louder, and that can be dangerous to a democracy."

"Raffie, I don't think you could have a democracy with only one party and with only one acceptable viewpoint."

"Accepting multiple viewpoints," Raffie continued, "has created many good things in our society, as long as it doesn't lead to violence. For example, Martin Luther King, Susan Anthony, Cesar Chavez, Abraham Lincoln, and John Lewis took up viable causes initially as nonmajority advocates. The results of their actions have been good for our country. But today it seems we have wannabe activists thinking they are like these revered agents of change. But they are just paper tigers blowing hot air in the wind, churning discontent, and causing chaos. Many are charlatans living off past societal transgressions and refreshing anew a period of discontent. Unfortunately, the young and easily persuaded people that come under their spells don't realize that the underlying problems they decry have mostly been addressed over the years."

The old man looked down at the ground again and said, "Paul, every solution to any major problem in our society must hinge on nonviolence. The elitists among us must understand that their means to affect change cannot be driven by deception, violent protest, and looting. The ends never justify the means when one resorts to violence or deception. Violent actions result in bitterness and contempt for the protesters. And if violence is committed, like destroying property and causing deaths, the protesters' desired change will move much slower, if at all."

I thought about his last words. I knew several times in history had proven the points he had made. "Revolutions are driven by violence," I said. "I don't think things are even close to being bad enough in this country to warrant any type of revolution."

"Paul, that's why moderation must be encouraged when protesters turn violent or begin looting. Sometimes the change is already in progress, and there is no need for violence or destructive protests. And pushing a flawed agenda too far in our country is not good for the elitists. The elitists should be mindful of what happened to the elite class in the French Revolution and in the overthrow of czarist Russia. Alexander Hamilton feared that revolutionaries do not know when to put the brakes on. Revolutionaries can be so idealistic that nothing is good enough. Ultimately, no one is capable of living up to their idealistic standards, and they turn on themselves. We don't want anarchism to gain a foothold in this country."

At that moment the screen door opened, and the old cowboy emerged with Miggy holding two bags full of groceries.

Miggy asked, "Manny, is it OK if I put these bags on the floor of your front seat?"

"That will be fine. It's unlocked."

Miggy moved adroitly down the steps carrying the two bags and managed to open the passenger door of the pickup, carefully placing the bags on the floorboard.

He returned to the porch and said to Manny, "Nothing should fall while you're driving. I braced everything between the seat and the dashboard."

The old cowboy nodded in appreciation. "Thanks, Miggy."

Miggy dutifully turned and went back inside the grocery.

The old cowboy smiled at us and asked us in his raspy western voice, "Well, gentlemen, did you solve all of the problems in our country yet?"

I answered first. "Not exactly. I might have to stay here a week or so to accomplish that feat."

Raffie added, chuckling, "A week or so? Maybe a year or two."

Manny reached for his back, and I could see that he winced in pain.

Raffie asked as he had before, "You sure I can't help you with the VA? There are people there I know that can help you."

"No, I don't need any help, Raffie. It was nice of you last year to try to get me some assistance for my growing disability, but I don't need any help. I returned the checks they sent me. I told them to keep the money and help others who are truly in need. I'm doing fine."

"Manny, I know you don't want any help," Raffie said. "And I understand fully where you are coming from. But you are entitled to some benefits. You earned them after thirty years in the military. You served our country and you're suffering now from ailments related to your service."

The old cowboy shook his head. "I got a military pension and a small postal service pension. I got my VA benefits as well. I don't need no more money from the Government. They've given me enough in my lifetime. And the Government already has spent more than they have. Why add to the shortfall? They need the money more than me."

I was shocked to hear Manny's response. I had never heard anyone turn down financial assistance from the government. Was he wrong in his beliefs? Was he foolish? Was he too genuine at being independent?

Manny looked at us and said, "My dad always told me no one owes you nothing in this world. And that's the way I look at it. I don't need help from the government other than what I'm already getting."

I nodded, understanding his position, but I had to question his logic. "That's admirable of you to turn down the financial help, but the government acknowledged they owed you the assistance for your disability. Why wouldn't you take the assistance?"

"I couldn't look at myself in the mirror if I took that government money when I'm doing just fine. I just couldn't. It's not right. It's how I was brought up."

I nodded slowly, still trying to understand.

Suddenly Manny turned toward the parking lot and, tipping his cowboy hat to the both of us, politely said, "Gentlemen, it's been a pleasure talking to you. And it was nice to meet you, Paul, but I have to get home to feed my chickens and cows. If you don't feed them at the same time every day they get a little ornery. And I don't want no broken fences."

The old cowboy tiresomely limped to the steps, and grabbing the railing, he slowly descended one step at a time. I watched as he retraced his steps to the old pickup truck and climbed inside. He looked at us through the semi-opaque windshield and feebly raised his hand to wave goodbye.

After he drove away, Raffie turned to me and said, "Manny is one of the few remaining out here who still lives by the old Code of the West. Paul, are you familiar with the Code of the West?"

"No, I don't know anything about that. I've heard of it but can't tell you what it is."

"The Code of the West was never written down, but it was shared from one generation to the next. The rugged pioneers were bound by it. The Code encouraged integrity, hard work, self-reliance, loyalty, and respect for others. That is why Manny said he was brought up that way. He can't change his core beliefs and be true to himself. Even when it's beneficial to him to do so."

I nodded now, understanding why Manny refused any more help. "Raffie, I have to say I respect him for being so independent and honest. I haven't met anyone like him before in my life. I guess he exemplifies a long-ago philosophy that is hard to live by today."

Raffie smiled. "If you could turn back time to two hundred years ago, that ole cowboy would perfectly fit in with the pioneers on the frontier. I don't doubt that one minute. He's one of a kind today, but he wouldn't have been unique two hundred years ago."

*****

I looked over at Raffie, and he seemed to be comfortably relaxing in his chair. His head was as far back as it would go as he watched each car and truck go by on the highway. Slowly he turned to me and said casually, "Politics is so funny. What is so amazing to me today is how each political party has morphed and flipped its base and sometimes parts of its platform to win elections. The middle-class workers, the rank and file, no longer favor the traditional party they used to belong to. The industrialists and intellectual elitists have migrated to the party that once only supported the common man and woman."

"Politics is indeed a strange animal," I said.

"Paul, how the parties define the have and the have-nots they represent is constantly changing."

The old man stopped to cough and clear his throat. Then he turned toward the screen door and called out, "Miggy, can you please bring Paul and me some water? My throat's getting dry. I appreciate it. Thanks."

In just a few seconds, Miggy suddenly appeared at the screen door with two bottles of water in hand. "Here you go," he said, handing the clear bottles of water to each of us. "Raffie, this should help your throat."

The old man carefully unscrewed the top of the water bottle and took a long drink. Miggy stood by, waiting for approbation.

"Oh, that tastes good. Thanks, Miggy—that helps a lot."

"Great. Anything more?" Miggy asked, looking at the both of us.

"Unless Paul wants something, I think we're fine."

I shook my head. "I don't need anything. Thanks for the water."

Miggy smiled contentedly and went back inside.

The old man took another long drink of water and then placed the bottle by his side in the chair. He turned to me and began again, "Paul, our country can indeed swing one way and then another along the political spectrum. When one approach is pushed too far and ultimately fails, as they all do eventually due to excesses, our nation usually will move back toward the center and sometimes even in the opposite direction to counter the excesses. But sometimes we see attempts to avoid allowing it to swing to the center. We cannot allow that to happen. We cannot allow a political ideology that needs self-correction to persist because of government interference. You know unchecked power and success in the political world bring arrogance and corruption, which ultimately lead to many other problems."

The old man stopped and reached down by his side and picked up the water bottle. He unscrewed the top and took another long drink from the bottle. "That water does wonders for my throat," he said. "My doctor told me I don't hydrate enough. She is right."

I watched as the old man ran the water bottle across his forehead, and I could see the glistening condensation above his brow. "Paul, we all get complacent when things in this country appear to be going well, and then we push it too far, and things start to not go so well. It's at these times, like now, that the pendulum swings back. Which is not a bad thing, as long as moderation prevails when it swings in the opposite direction. But this only happens in a free democracy, where the consensus of the citizens can change the direction of a nation without applying force to do so."

Suddenly I felt the familiar buzzing vibration in my pocket from my cell phone. I pulled it out, looked down to read the screen, and saw it was my wife calling. I slowly got up and turned to the old man and said, "Raffie, I'm sorry to interrupt our conversation. I've got to take this call. It's my wife. I'll be back in a minute."

The old man nodded. "You must always take a call from your wife. She's the boss, right?"

I smiled with a nod and excused myself. I went around to the side of Miggy's grocery to have more privacy.

Once around the corner of the building, I began speaking into the phone. "Hey, honey. I'm still here in Las Cruces. The rental car should be fixed and back on the road in time to get me to Albuquerque. If that all happens, I should be able to catch the last flight out and be home tonight."

She answered cheerfully, "Great. Paul Junior has a soccer match tomorrow morning, and Krista can't wait to show you what she made."

"I'm sure I'll be surprised at what Krista made. She is so creative."

"Well, you better be surprised, or at least look like it. She's quite proud of it."

"Don't worry—I will be surprised. I guess I'll grab a bite here before I get out of town."

"Oh, Paul, also your dad called during lunch and wants you to go up to the lake house next weekend. I think he's lonely and wants someone to fish with him. It's not a bad idea if we all go. We have no baseball or soccer games next weekend. I'm sure the kids would like to swim and enjoy the hiking. And up there it should be a little more comfortable."

"I'd like more comfortable. It's too hot here. Just standing here in the sun it feels like a hundred twenty degrees."

Along the side of Miggy's grocery, there was only open sunlight. I could feel the heat radiating from the ground through the soles of my shoes. Looking behind Miggy's grocery, I saw there were no trees or shade there either, only scrub-like foliage dotting the large, dusty back lot.

"Paul, make sure you drink plenty of water. It's so easy to get dehydrated in that weather. You dehydrate before you know it because you don't sweat."

"Yes, I know. I have been drinking some water." I walked farther down the side of the building, trying to cool my feet off. "There's a nice old guy here who is really interesting to talk to. An incredible older guy."

"That's good. I'm sure having someone to pass the time with makes it a little easier while you are waiting for the car to be fixed."

"Leah, this guy is really smart, and he's done a lot of things in his life. We've been talking about the country and his life growing up. He has quite a story, not boring at all."

"Well, good. I've got to go pick up Krista now from school. I'll be at the airport tonight. I checked your flight, and your departure is still on schedule. Paul, remember—be surprised with what Krista made. And don't forget to drink enough water. Love you."

"Honey, I will. Leah, if Dad calls back, tell him we'll go to the lake house next weekend. Love you too."

As I came back around the building, I saw Miggy coming out the screen door with a couple of candy bars in hand. As I approached the steps, Miggy said, "Raffie likes a little pick-me-up after lunch, and he always has a candy bar. I brought one out for you as well. Do you like chocolate?"

I looked at Miggy and smiled. "Well, yes, I do. I could use a little pick-me-up. Thanks."

I watched as the old man slowly unwrapped the candy bar he was holding in his hand. "You are great, Migg," he said appreciatively. "And as always, you're right on the spot."

I was relieved to be back up on the porch, under the shade. "Raffie, I'm amazed how hot the sand is out there. The heat ran right through the soles of my shoes."

The old man smiled and said, "Now you know why only young men can work in this heat. And by the way, in this heat your chocolate candy bar will melt pretty quickly."

I reached down and picked up my bottle of water from the floor of the deck. I bent my head backward and with huge gulps heartily drank from the bottle. I am not enamored with flavorless water, but when I am really thirsty, it tastes better than anything in the world. It was refreshing, and immediately I felt a pickup in focus and alertness. I rubbed the cool plastic bottle across my forehead, hoping to get additional relief from the heat.

The old man was watching me as I cooled myself off with the bottle of water. "Paul, have you ever heard of the rule of three?"

I shook my head. "No, I can't say that I have."

"Well, at best you can only live for three minutes without breathing air and oxygen. You can live three weeks without food. And last, you can live only three days without water."

"I bet you wouldn't last three days out here without water," I said drily.

*****

A little while later, a 1960s classic convertible pulled off the road and parked along the highway in front of Miggy's. I thought it was odd that the automobile had stopped out at the side of the highway and had not pulled fully into the parking lot in front of the porch.

The car was long and wide and could dwarf any car made today. It was the type of car I had seen on television automobile auction shows, but this one had not been restored. I could see it had been driven hard and abused a bit. There was a thick, permanently stained coating of dust and pollen caked over the hood and roof.

Three young men wearing sleeveless T-shirts climbed out. Two of the young men had long, stringy hair, and the third, who loitered near the car, had a short haircut with the sides shaved evenly around his head. All three had the beginnings of thin mustaches with goatees. Their facial hair was not well pronounced or coarse and appeared at a distance to be more like rough stubble. I figured they were probably in their late teens or early twenties based on their physique and stride. All three wore sunglasses and ball caps pulled down low over their foreheads.

I watched as the two young men approached the porch. They did not look up, and they appeared to be avoiding any eye contact. I turned to look at Raffie, who was watching them. I could see that Raffie was also looking past them to the one standing by the car. I could see that the young man waiting at the car was looking down the road, and just as abruptly he turned his head to look in the other direction. From a distance, he seemed nervous and was moving side to side as if anticipating a foreboding event.

Raffie slowly cleared his throat as the young men approached. Speaking in a clear, commanding voice, he asked, "You guys from around here?"

The taller of the two hesitated and then answered, "We came here on a trip."

The taller young man had a large tattoo on his arm that looked like a flying phoenix. It had multiple colors and was very pronounced. I noticed for the first time that he was carrying something in a small brown bag he held tightly to his side so as not to let it be observable.

"On a trip?" Raffie asked inquisitively. "Where are you going?"

The tall young man at first looked like he was not going to answer the question, but finally he relented and mumbled, "Got relatives north of here."

I looked at the other teen, who remained quiet. He was rocking slightly back and forth. He seemed to be unsettled. When I looked at him, he turned his head and looked away. He stayed right behind the taller young man and seemed to be trying not to be too conspicuous.

The taller young man started to reach for the door, and Raffie said, "Your friend seems anxious out there by the street. Is he OK?"

The taller young man pulled his hand slowly away from the doorknob. Still keeping his head down, he backed up a step, almost colliding with the other young man standing behind him. He answered abruptly, "He's always anxious and nervous. It's just him."

Raffie asked, "You boys have jobs?"

The shorter young man suddenly answered with a noticeable anxiety in his voice, blurting out his words. "We don't have jobs. We come from El Paso and need work. We never been in trouble or anything. We got no money left."

The taller young man turned and flashed a look of frustration and anger at the other teen, shaking his head at his companion who had spoken up. He stepped again toward the door, and Raffie interjected, "So you need money?"

The shorter young man spoke up again. "We just used our last bit of money to put some gas in the car to get this far."

The taller young man turned around now to the other and admonished him in a stern tone, "Shut up, man. Keep your mouth shut." He seemed a bit jittery now and less composed, and he began moving the bag that he was holding along his side up and down.

Raffie asked, "What's in the bag?"

The taller man hesitated again to answer, and clutching the bag tightly to his side, he suddenly looked away and said, "Nothing you need to know about."

The shorter young man spoke up again. "We need to find some work. We haven't worked for over three months."

Raffie looked at the two men. I could see he was studying their faces. He asked, "What would you say if I found all of you jobs?"

The two young men looked at each other. The taller young man turned now and looked at Raffie. His fortress demeanor seemed to relent slightly, and he asked in an abrupt tone, "Doing what?"

The third young man at the street now let out a brief whistling sound, and the two young men on the deck turned, looking momentarily at him. A few seconds later, a car whizzed by.

Raffie said, "I have a friend who could put you to work tomorrow with factory jobs in Tucson. These would be good jobs. Steady work if you want to work."

The taller young man did not speak right away. He seemed to be thinking for a moment, and then he asked inquisitively, in a suspicious, doubtful tone, "Factory jobs? What do we have to do? And what does it pay?"

I sensed at this moment that Raffie had defused whatever their intention had originally been. They now seemed curious about Raffie's offer. They both stood still, looking at Raffie, waiting for his response.

"It's a job putting auto parts together. A lot of machining. They would take you three on and train you. It's a good job."

The taller young man asked apprehensively, still with a suspicious, questioning tone in his voice, "But how much does it pay? We would be inexperienced workers. We've never had factory jobs."

"I can't answer that exactly. But the last young person I sent up there two years ago is making twice the minimum wage and then some. He's actually going to school at night and stays in contact with me."

The shorter young man spoke again before the taller young man could speak. "But how do we get there? We got no more money. We can't even buy gas to get there."

Raffie smiled at the young men. "If you are interested in getting jobs, I can take care of that."

The two looked at each other again, and the taller young man answered, "Yeah, I think we are interested. But why do you care about helping us? No one has ever helped us like this before."

Raffie sat back in his chair and answered, "I like to help people. I want young people to make the right decisions in their lives and be successful. I don't want to see young people do things that are harmful to themselves. Like making big mistakes that lead to real bad consequences. Consequences that could ruin their lives. That's why I want to help you boys. If you have no money or jobs, what are you going to do next? I don't want you to get into trouble."

I watched as the taller young man stepped forward, and suddenly a slow but brief smile appeared on his face. He looked at Raffie as if he now understood the old man's intention. Then he said in a calmer and more appreciative voice, "Yes, mister, we are interested in those jobs. We would like to have factory jobs in Tucson."

"Good. Let me call my friend first," Raffie quickly responded. "You boys wait out at your car, and I'll let you know. It won't take long."

The young men turned and looked at each other again, and the taller motioned his companion toward the steps, taking the lead. The other young man obediently followed him.

Raffie fumbled for his phone as the boys walked back to the car parked on the edge of the highway. I was wondering what he was going to do. Was he going to call a friend or alert the authorities to what might be happening? But I knew Raffie was a friend in need, and I thought that, being a man of his word, he truly would help these young men.

The old man hit several buttons on his phone. I could see the young men at the street now looking at him. I couldn't tell if they trusted Raffie completely or not.

"Hey, George, it's Raffie. How are you are doing?"

Raffie listened and then asked, "I have three young men here who are in need of jobs. Can you do me a favor and find a position for them? Take care of them?"

Raffie listened and slowly nodded. "Well, thank you, George. That's a huge favor you'd do for me. And they're going to need training. They've never worked in a factory setting. They don't have any factory skills. I'm going to send them your way tonight." Raffie stopped to check his watch. "They'll probably be there around seven or so tonight if they get a start now."

Raffie listened again and added, "Start them out at what you paid Alex. And just to be safe, run a background check on each of them as well. Thank you, George."

The old man put the cell phone down and slowly motioned to the young men to come back up on the porch. This time all three came together, striding eagerly, with a sudden sense of urgency in their step.

I turned and watched the old man as he sat comfortably in his chair. He was relaxed and was sitting up as straight as his body would allow him to. He made a hand motion to summon the young men up to the deck, and it reminded me of a pontiff giving his benevolent blessings to these young men.

As they approached, Raffie asked, "Do any of you have a piece of paper I can write on?"

The young man who had been at the car fumbled through his back pocket and pulled out a scrap of paper that he carefully unfolded. I could see the paper was worn on the edges and had writing on it. He gingerly handed it to Raffie and said, "I know it's a bit used. Will this do?"

The old man took the paper and studied it for a second. He nodded that it was acceptable. He fumbled in his front shirt pocket and pulled out a pen. I watched Raffie's wrinkled hand, covered in brown age spots, slowly moving the pen. The pen didn't work at first, and the old man scribbled in circles on the paper until the ink appeared.

He wrote for several seconds and then handed the paper to the taller teen. "Here is the factory address in Tucson, and ask for George—he knows me. Tell him Raffie sent you. And he knows you're coming tonight to see him. I've also included his phone number in case you get lost."

The young men nodded in unison. As they acknowledged Raffie's kindness, I could tell they were more relaxed, and their appearance was more sociable. The shorter young man who had originally come up to the porch said, "Mister, I didn't know what we were going to do. But we are all thankful to you for helping us."

The taller young man spoke up now. His voice sounded much more contrite, without even a hint of suspicion or defiance. "Mister, I appreciate you doing this for us. We didn't expect anyone to help us here, but you have. I just want to say thank you. No one ever helped us like this before."

The third young man standing behind them nodded his head slowly in agreement.

"Boys, you're welcome. I realize that you are going to need some money to get there." The old man slowly reached into his back pocket, took out his worn leather wallet, and produced several one-hundred-dollar bills. "This should get you boys there and settled. George will take care of you. He and I have been in business for many years. If you leave now, you should get there just before dusk."

The young men stood on the deck without moving, looking down at the old man's hand and the crisp, new one-hundred-dollar bills. I think seeing the cash in hand suddenly struck home to them that all this was indeed real and was going to happen. The tall young man stepped forward, took the bills, and put them in the front pocket of his jeans. A broad smile now broke across his face. "Thank you again, Mr. Raffie."

The three turned now and walked back toward their car. I observed that their stride was more upright than before, and they walked with their heads up. There was a sense of pride and confidence in their step, and I sensed they were no longer anxious about their future.

The old man called after them. "Don't disappoint me. This is a great opportunity for all of you. George will teach you a lot. Remember—tell him that Raffie sent you."

They responded together in chorus, "Thank you again."

As they reached their car along the roadside, one of the young men turned around and promised, "We will not disappoint you and we'll learn and do a good job. Sir, have a good day."

The large classic automobile backed up slowly, and as it pulled away through a cloud of dust, several hands waved from outside the windows. As they accelerated down the road, I could see stones bouncing on the highway behind them, catapulted from the wheels.

*****

The afternoon's relentless sun baked the highway and radiated heat in shimmering waves. As I sat there looking across the highway, I noted how the rising broiling heat from the asphalt bent and distorted my view. The distortions appeared as disjointed images, sliced apart and reconnected out of order like objects in an impressionist painting. I gauged the feel-like temperature to be now well over a hundred degrees. And yet we still had not reached the peak temperature of the day. I looked at the old man and noticed again that he did not seem to be affected by the heat. He was content sitting there and staring at the highway, watching the traffic pass by in front of the grocery.

Raffie began now to reposition himself in his chair. I could see it was a struggle to get his back and legs to move in unison, and he pushed the floor of the deck, trying to slide backward to straighten up. His gray tasseled hair moved slightly as a gust of warm wind invaded the porch.

"Paul, as an old man, I can't complain," he began, smiling to himself. "I've been blessed so many times in my life. I've had to make many decisions in my life as to which road to travel. As I look back on it now, I can see times where I could have gone in a completely different direction. But by the grace of God, I made the right decisions. I've hurdled most of the roadblocks."

The old man looked up at the ceiling of the porch and continued to reflect on his life's journey. "In my time on this earth, as with everyone else, there have been some things I could control, but there were many things that happened that were out of my control. I could describe the uncontrollable events that turned out positive as fortuitous or lucky, or maybe just a matter of having good karma. But I see them all as divine blessings."

He stopped to clear his throat and continued in the same reflective tone. "Paul, I must confess there were things I did in my youth that today I am not proud of and would do differently. Not major things but things I might have said or not said to people in my life." The old man turned toward me now, and a slow smile crept across his face. "Don't ever believe anyone who tells you that they would never do anything different in their lives if they could go back in time. Everyone has said things or done things they wish they hadn't said or done."

Raffie stopped now and looked off into the distance. "Paul, there were choices I made in my blind youth that I thought were right, and I was so sure they were right. But looking back, I know they would not have been good choices. I was dating a girl when I was in my early twenties—I was so sure I wanted to marry her. But what a mistake that would have been. Neither of us had any idea what we wanted or how our lives would have been different if we got married. In hindsight, the relationship would have ended in a few years and would have set both of our lives back to a restart. And then I met the right girl, and everything was right and good, and our lives over the years grew together and intertwined, you know, like the roots of an old banyan tree. Paul, have you ever seen the roots of a banyan tree?"

"Yes, I have, Raffie. Once in southwest Florida I saw one. The tree had roots that extended above the ground in each direction at least thirty yards. And the roots were all intertwined."

"Just like Marcia and me—we were intertwined. We were destined to be together."

*****

Raffie sat for a while quietly in his chair as if he were absorbing the atmosphere around him. I could hear him inhaling and exhaling deeply. Suddenly he began again. "I think if a young person can achieve the age of twenty-five without getting into any major trouble or screwing up their life, the remaining years will bode well for them."

Ruminating on the old man's words got me thinking about my youthful indiscretions. I could remember some of the ridiculous and irrational things I said and did when I was young. However, I didn't make any major mistakes in my youth, and I survived past my twenty-fifth birthday abundantly unblemished. But the foolish things I said and did in my youth—and there were many—I still do regret. I wince when I think now about some of those things. Things I did that I would never divulge or confide to anyone today. Hopefully, over time the memory of those events will fade away and seem less embarrassing.

"Paul, before one reaches twenty-five years old, decisions are often based more on personal feelings, peer pressure, and sometimes unchecked desires. They are not often based on personal experiences or fully utilizing any critical thinking. Critical thinking in life is very important. It can cut down on the number of bad decisions made. Young people need to be taught about critical thinking. Especially today, when so much disinformation, misinformation, abject propaganda, and commercial messaging occurs."

As I listened to Raffie, I did not fully understand what he meant by *critical thinking*, so I asked him, "You mentioned that critical thinking is imperative for a young person trying to make better decisions in their life. But how does it work, and how do you teach it?"

"Ah, Paul, critical thinking isn't hard. You don't have to be a genius to understand it or to use it. And by the way, it is very important in a vibrant democracy as well to have critical thinkers. When anyone reads or hears something that may be too good to be true or is highly biased or slanted, they need to question each statement presented. Especially statements that include assumptions, guarantees, or any promises regarding an absolute outcome."

"OK, I understand that," I said. "It's a discipline, like peeling the layers of an onion to get to the truth."

"Exactly. To fully utilize critical thinking, a person must also question and challenge not only the message but also the motive of the messenger. Are they knowledgeable about the subject matter? Are they trying to push their own opinion on you? Are they biased? Do they receive any benefit from their persuasion? One must look behind the curtain and understand the motive of the messenger. This does not mean everyone who is biased or pushing their opinion on you is conveying misinformation or disinformation. For example, maybe a young person might wish to pursue a career in a specific profession. He or she may ask several individuals in that profession what they like and don't like about their profession. It does not mean the individuals providing the answers cannot be taken at their word, especially when their statements may be their opinions only. But the young person will need to utilize some critical thinking in the decision process. The individuals' opinions presented as facts will need to be further questioned for a deeper knowledge of the profession. Follow-up questions, along with valid research, will be needed to gain a wider and firmer understanding of the profession. And that is very important when one is making a lifelong career decision."

"Raffie, I can definitely see how today, with all the messaging we get, everyone needs critical thinking skills."

The old man slowly nodded and said, "And this is especially true today with all the conflicting messages and news stories we are continually bombarded with. Today journalists sometimes act as activists, and their motives and viewpoints need to be analyzed and questioned. They often allow, consciously or subconsciously, their biased viewpoints to creep into their articles, sometimes even shading or softening the truth. And even worse, opposing viewpoints are sometimes never presented or are buried deep in their articles. But critical thinking can help unearth the validity of the message or its deception.

"Paul, here's another example of critical thinking. Let's say someone is asked, 'Why did you vote for candidate A?' If the answer is 'Because I only vote for candidates from a specific party,' or 'I heard candidate B said this or that' through a filtered media, or 'I think candidate A is nice and attractive,' that is not an answer informed by critical thinking. The person's response sounds good, but the person didn't answer why they will only vote for candidate A. Candidate A may be a nice person, and their party platform might seem attractive, but are they the best candidate? Are they truthful? What is their track record? Do they overpromise and underdeliver? Have the things they've done actually improved your standard of living? If the voter applies some critical thinking to the decision process, they might actually realize candidate B is a better choice than candidate A."

"Raffie, that makes sense to me. Decisions should be made more on the basis of facts than feelings and fuzzy thinking."

"Paul, Aristotle way back when considered logic the tool or instrument of the sciences. Critical thinking requires the use of logic to discern the truth, which can lead to the best solutions to problems. Wrong decisions will still be made, but they should be fewer."

At this point I was thinking to myself. I recalled several students in college that were very logical in their thought and approach to life. In many respects I admired them and thought they acted mature beyond their years. When others were partying and having fun, they were committed to their studies. One colleague I remembered wanted a career in robotics, and after graduating with an advanced engineering degree, he applied to and got accepted at a prominent technology school to continue his research development work. I was always impressed with him, as he was so singularly focused and disciplined. I must admit I wasn't like that in school.

"Paul, patience is so important in making good, logical decisions. If one has the time, important decisions should not be hurried. Few things in life happen in a hurry. I thank my mom and dad every day for instilling in me the desire to stay focused on leading a good life and to work hard at it. I found out early on as a young man that life is difficult. The pitfalls of youth are many, and the defenses are few."

I nodded in agreement and commented, "My dad used to say there is no substitute for hard work. You might not be the best at something you are doing, but if you have some ability and work harder than everyone else, you will be recognized and stand out from the crowd."

"Yes, working hard and having ability, tempered with persistence, are important in achieving your dreams." The old man stopped for a second, and I could see that he was watching something at some distance in the sky. I turned and saw far away a pair of vultures circling underneath the clouds. The vultures drifted at different altitudes, riding the updrafts of warm air emanating from the prairie. I wondered what they were circling over.

The old man looked down at the deck floor and began again, "Paul, I was presented with many opportunities along the road that would have led to dead ends. Some of the opportunities promised great rewards and a quick road to a successful utopia. Fortunately, thank God, I didn't take the bait. The promises were unrealistic and would never have materialized. It taught me in life to be patient. I had to avoid the alluring voices of the sirens. I had to think critically. Most people expect to get their rewards right away, but life seldom works that way."

"Like those that try to get rich quick," I pointed out. "A lot of people fall into that trap today."

The old man slowly nodded. "Yeah, there are no easy roads in achieving success and accomplishing your dreams. Nothing worth achieving in life is easy. Like a happy marriage, a stable family, a good education, and a good job making a living."

I smiled and added, "And if taking shortcuts got you any further, everybody would already be doing it."

"And Paul, the rewards would be much less."

*****

Raffie tilted up his water bottle and took a long drink. I could see bubbles rising to the mouth of the bottle as he gulped down the water. Then he placed the bottle beside him in his lap. "Paul, I believe one of the hardest decisions a young person has to make is to determine what they are good at."

"I know I struggled with that before I got into banking. I thought I'd be a great engineer or a major-league baseball player growing up, but I wasn't equipped for either of those professions. I quit fooling myself when I received my first low grade in college, in statics. And when I wasn't drafted out of a youth baseball league."

"It's not easy to determine what you are good at and what you are meant to do," the old man responded. "Sometimes the arrogance of youth fools itself. Finding a career can be an iterative process. You would think a young person would consult with their parents, but young people don't necessarily like to get advice from their parents."

I laughed. "I know. I'm a father."

"Paul, a career-minded young person should go out and find someone they trust who has made a similar decision to the one that they are contemplating. Try to find someone who went down that same road they want to go down. Find out what made that person choose that path. Listen to what mistakes they made and what they did to achieve their dreams. But most important, the young person must listen, really listen with an open mind. Then, with all that information in mind, they need to spend some time alone. They need to think clearly through the decision and process all the facts. What is the upside, and what is the downside? Can they easily recover if the downside occurs? Are they willing to make the sacrifice to achieve the desired goal? In all this process, they need to be utilizing critical thinking."

I smiled. "Most people don't think that way. They want a specific outcome but refuse to see the reality of what it takes to get there."

"Paul, again, I don't want you to think that I believe people shouldn't take some chances in life. Sometimes it is a leap of faith. But they do need to make sure there is a safety net and escape plan if their decision fails. If plan A doesn't work, you better have a backup plan. Look at me—I started out as a geologist in the field, and when it didn't work for me, I started working on a rig and was much happier."

"Raffie, I think some people give up before they reach their goals or dreams."

"Yes, some people get right up to the edge of achieving their dreams and just quit. They give up. And that's a shame. Especially when the decision to end their journey is solely driven by an emotional issue or interpersonal issues. Everything may be in line for them to reach their goal, but they self-destruct. They can't get along with others, or they just don't have the drive or hardened exterior to persist against the naysayers. They may need a harder shell, like a turtle."

I laughed and quipped, "Raffie, I can tell you've given a lot of thought to this. I think you could have been a life coach! You would have been a great career counselor at a school."

The old man chuckled at my humorous suggestion. "Paul, I hope I'm not boring you with all this."

"No, I find it quite interesting."

"Paul, I've also given some thought to this point. Young people need to be mindful of conventional wisdom, but they should not always rely on it. Reality sometimes crashes through conventional wisdom. Critical thinking can help a lot here. Friends and family might discourage you and try to convince you that you can't do something. That your dreams are possible but your place in society makes them impossible. That society will always prevent you from achieving your dreams. Remember, at one time conventional wisdom was that the earth could only be flat. The majority of people held that as a truth, and at the time, that made perfect sense. But if one follows conventional wisdom without questioning and challenging it, one may never achieve one's full opportunity in life. Columbus would never have gone sailing west if he thought he would fall off the earth."

I asked, "But conventional wisdom is not always wrong. Isn't it true that if you don't study you can't get into college? And if you are constantly reckless you will eventually get hurt?"

"Yes, Paul, sometimes there are elements of conventional wisdom that are universally true and have been since the dawn of man. But a contrarian example would be that no one from a poor family can achieve anything in our society because they are disadvantaged. Another would be that women can't be good firefighters or police officers. I would argue that there are many examples where conventional wisdom was wrong. Conventional wisdom can be an ever-changing process, and it can sometimes be proven wrong over time. Young people should never let conventional wisdom deter them from their goals or define them and prevent them from doing what they are capable of doing. Yes, it can be harder for the economically and socially disadvantaged to achieve their full potential—but not impossible. At least not in our society."

The old man continued now with an ever more convincing tone in his voice, "However, I am a strong, strong, strong believer in common sense. Everything has a cause and effect. If you do something that surely will lead to a negative outcome, you are not using common sense. If I step off a ten-story building and expect not to fall, I'm not using common sense. Sometimes common sense and conventional wisdom intersect. But common sense is more supported by science, experience, universal truth, and history. One can unearth common sense through the process of critical thinking. But sometimes it may take some digging."

"Unfortunately," I said smiling, "today we need more common sense in politics and in Washington."

"I would agree common sense is becoming very rare in Washington. Politicians often push laws to satisfy their base. Sometimes even to buy votes that have negative consequences. It is very important in a democracy that commonsense lawmakers incorporate an understanding of the human elements of society—like what drives selfishness, greed, laziness, and the other bad aspects of human nature. Conversely, they need to fully understand what drives positive behaviors in our society."

The old man stopped and slightly coughed into his elbow. "We live in a country where some politicians in Washington seem to be trying to take away our cherished liberties piece by piece. Isn't that what the British did to the colonies? Isn't that what the Soviet Union did? Common sense would say that destroying dissident viewpoints and a sense of individualism will eventually lead to tyranny and create a threat to our democracy. The citizens will feel they are voiceless, and they will become apathetic. Apathy among the voting public can be very destructive to a democratic republic. It can lead to less motivation and a decline in productivity, which will inevitably result in a decline in the standard of living. Conventional wisdom would say that no one will ever challenge the status quo, as the government can use propaganda, the threat of imprisonment, and excessive force against its dissidents. But in a thriving, healthy democracy, we can self-correct these mistakes and reverse harms that have been committed. Individual rights can be restored, and all voices and viewpoints can and must be heard."

*****

I suddenly heard the screeching of brakes and the loud, sustained blast of a car horn. I looked up to see what was happening and quickly located the source of the commotion. A car turning left into Miggy's parking lot had turned in front of a westbound car, forcing the driver to hit the brakes to avoid a collision. I could see that the westbound car had now pulled off the road and had come to an abrupt stop along the roadside just down from Miggy's parking lot. The driver inside the car was clearly shaken from the close encounter and was resting his head on the steering wheel. The other car, the one that had created the near miss, had slowly veered into the parking lot and had come to a coasting stop just short of the porch. The smell of burning brake pads and burnt rubber filled the air.

I studied the car in front of me that was sitting within a few feet of the porch. It was an older-model silver car that needed some bodywork. The driver-side headlight was broken, and the adjacent door panel was creased in. There were also several deep scratches along the hood of the car, and the front grill and bumper were pitted with several dents. Given how the driver had just avoided a collision while turning into the parking lot, I assumed all the damage to the exterior of the car was the result of previous accidents.

As I was looking at the car parked in front of me, the driver's door slowly opened. A rather rough-looking middle-aged man appeared to be struggling, trying to get out of the car. As he leaned out of the vehicle, he must have caught his leg on the threshold of the door. His body awkwardly tumbled from behind the open car door to the ground. His fall was like a slow-motion video, and when he hit the ground, a cloud of dust flipped up around him. I watched as the disoriented man sat there a few seconds without moving on the silty sand parking lot. There was a look of bewilderment on his face, as if he was trying to understand where he was and why he was sitting on the ground. As he slowly gathered the reality of his situation, he appeared ambivalent about his predicament, almost nonchalant, as if whatever had just happened or was happening to him did not matter. As I looked beside him, I noticed two empty beer cans on the ground that had followed him during his fall from the car.

I watched as the man slowly attempted to stand up, grappling onto the open driver's side door as a brace. After some difficulty and several failed attempts, he finally got to his feet and began halfheartedly slapping his shirt and pants, attempting to remove the dust. His efforts to clean himself up were fruitless and almost seemed comical. As he stood there, I noticed his clothes looked well worn. He was wearing a white T-shirt with holes in the sleeves and an old pair of faded jeans. His shoes appeared weathered with creases, and I could see visible tears and cracks in the leather. His graying beard was uneven and scraggly. His hair was tousled back and forth and looked as if he had just rolled out of bed. My kids would have told me he had a bad case of bed head.

The disheveled-looking man now seemed to be trying to gather his bearings. He started to move sideways at first and then suddenly corrected his direction and began to move in a more direct path toward the porch. He kept his head down, concentrating on his efforts to move forward one step at a time. As he trudged forward, I could see he was swaying left and right. His face now appeared to have a look of focused determination. Upon reaching the steps, he stopped for a moment. It appeared as if he was attempting to contemplate his next move. The man looked at the steps and then down at his feet. He had a puzzled look on his face, as if walking up steps was new to him.

At this moment the man who was in the westbound car had gotten out of his vehicle and was walking swiftly across the parking lot toward the porch. I could see from his hurrying stride that he was going to be confrontational.

"Mister, mister," he yelled to the bewildered man who was now attempting to negotiate the first step up to the porch. "I want to talk to you."

The disheveled man abruptly turned around on the first step. Fumbling for the railing, he almost fell backward. He appeared to be looking with glassy eyes for the source of the yelling but did not seem to acknowledge the man coming stridently toward him.

As the other driver reached the porch, he began yelling in an obstreperous, angry tone, "Mister, you almost caused a serious accident. I could have been killed by that move of yours. You didn't see me coming toward you on the road? How could you have missed me?"

The haggard-looking man finally acknowledged the presence of the other driver and answered in disbelief, "What? What are you talking about? I didn't have no accident. Am I…" He stopped and began to slur his words. "I…I just come here to git sometin' to drink."

The other man retorted, "To drink? I think you've already had enough, judging from what you just did. You shouldn't be on the road. You are dangerous, man. You shouldn't be driving at all."

"I can't drive?" the drunk man answered belligerently, bracing himself on the railing so as not to fall. "Why not?

You can't tell me I can't drive. I have a right to drive. Just who are you?"

The other driver answered loudly in the face of the inebriated man, "You're a mess, man. Just look at yourself. I can't believe you are driving on the road. Don't you know you could hurt someone or yourself?"

"Nobody can tell me I can't drive," the inebriated man defiantly responded. "I can do whatever I want. I'm a grown man. You don't have a right to tell me I can't drive."

At this point the man yelling at the inebriated driver threw his arms up in the air in frustration and said, "No talking to you drunks. I'm wasting my time. You should be in jail as far as I'm concerned." He then turned around and began marching back to his car. As he walked away, he was shaking his head in anger and talking to himself in a loud tone. "Old drunk should get off the road. He's a menace to every driver and needs to have his license taken away."

I watched as the other driver got in his car now and drove away, still shaking his head in anger.

I could see the old man looking at the drunk man as he stood there on the deck. "Son, don't you think you've had enough to drink today?" he asked in a fatherly, calm voice.

The man stopped and looked toward Raffie. "Old man, jut sit thar and don't worry abot me."

"Son, I think you've had enough. I'm not going to let you leave here. Do you understand? You could hurt someone, and you could also hurt yourself."

The man suddenly raised his voice in anger, looking at Raffie. "Why you bothering me? I haven't dun nothing wrong to hurt you. Just leave me alone, old man."

Raffie turned and called through the front door, "Mig, don't let this man buy anything more to drink. He's had enough."

Miggy responded from inside, "I understand. Nothing more, Raffie."

"You can't do that," the man said again with anger in his voice. "I can go down the street to the Rancho Bar and get sometin'. Why you think you can stop me?"

Raffie did not answer but continued to look at the man. Then he turned toward the door again and said, "Mig, see if Rudy is nearby. He can assist this man here."

Again, Miggy responded from inside, "OK, will do. He should be around here someplace."

Raffie asked the man, "Son, why don't you sit down here and tell me about yourself. Just come over here and sit down."

The man seemed to be confused now and disconcerted. "Talk to you abot myself? What for? I don't need to talk to you."

"I just want to know more about you. I want to hear what you do for a living and where you live."

"What for?" the man asked. "Nobody cares abot me! My wife, my kids, my boss. Everybody has let me down. I got nothin' to say."

"Son, just have a seat and let's talk," Raffie said calmly. "I have to know more about you."

The man seemed reluctant to sit down, and Raffie asked again, "Son, just have a seat and tell me about yourself. I need for you to talk to me."

As I watched, the man's shoulders seemed to suddenly slump down in contrition. He looked toward the chair beside Raffie and said, "OK, maybe…but only for a minute. I got to get sometin' here. I can't wait. I got to get sometin' to drink."

Raffie patted the arm of the chair next to him to direct him where to sit. The man moved gingerly to the chair and finally sat down. "Now what?" he asked, looking at Raffie. "You got me in this damn char now."

Raffie smiled. "It's not an electric chair. It's not going to hurt you to sit here and talk."

I laughed at Raffie's comment and continued to listen to and watch the old man as he kept speaking to the inebriated man in a calm, fatherly tone.

"What's your name?"

"Lucas."

"Lucas, where do you live?"

"Just south of Rincon. Out in the country."

"Lucas, are you married? Do you have a wife and family around here?"

The man seemed to be suddenly annoyed at the questioning and answered, "No, not no more. She and the kids left me. I haven't seen them in years."

"Lucas, I'm sorry to hear that. What do you do for a living?"

"I git government assistance, and I work part-time when I can. I'm a framer. Build homes. I'm a damn good framer. But I haven't worked for a while."

Raffie seemed to be progressively trying to glean from the man an understanding of his situation in life. I wasn't quite sure yet why he wanted this information. So far, the man's life sounded pretty destitute and sad.

"Lucas, are your parents still living?"

"Naw, they died years ago. They left me a trailer I've been livin' in now fer over fifteen years."

The man now seemed to be less combative and more open as he spoke. "I gat a job next week on a house up the road. I don't know if I can do it anymore. I'm worried."

"Worried?" Raffie asked.

"Yeah, I gat to work at least eight hours a day. But I gat to be able to get away some during the day and be by myself. I gat the jitters if I don't."

"I understand," Raffie said. "I have a brother who is like you. You know you can change?"

The man laughed. "I'm havin' fun. I'm OK. I don't need to change."

"Lucas, when did you start drinking?"

"Today? Or when did I start to drink?"

Raffie cleared his throat. "In the beginning."

"Oh, let me think." The man pondered for a moment. "Probably ninth grade off and on."

"So you've been drinking for over thirty years?

"Yeah, that's about right." The man paused and looked down at the deck floor. "My dad drank a lot. I suppose he probably drank himself to death. I was in high school when he died. He was a strict disciplinarian. You never talked back to him, and none of us when we wer kids showed any disrespect to him. He beat me up pretty bad a few times for talking back. You know, it still sticks in my craw today."

"Lucas, did you ever want to stop drinking?"

The man paused and looked toward the street. "I suppose thar wer times. But I can't now."

"Son, I really want to help you. But I know you have to be willing to change."

"I'm having fun," he answered, laughing. "I don't need to change. I git by and don't need much."

A silver-and-black police car pulled up in the parking lot, and a tall, thin officer stepped out of the car. Raffie saw the police car and turned to the inebriated man and said, "Lucas, this is Officer Rudy coming here. I know him. You have to understand I can't let you get back in your car. It's too dangerous. I'm going to see what we can do for you."

The man turned to Raffie and suddenly protested in an angry tone, "Why did you call the police on me? That's not right. I don't want to go back to jail. Man, I trusted you."

"Lucas, calm down. This man can help you. Just stay calm."

The officer slowly walked up the steps. I noticed his uniform looked custom tailored and the creases in his sleeves and pants were well pressed. My guess was he was probably well over six feet tall, and he presented an imposing figure.

"Hey, Raffie," he said. "I understand you need some help?"

Raffie turned to the man sitting beside him. "Officer Rudy, this is Lucas. He lives near Rincon, and he's had a bit too much to drink today. I'm trying to save him from making a big mistake if he gets back on the road."

The officer looked at the man and immediately sighed. "Yes, I know Lucas Simpson. He is not supposed to be driving anymore. You said he was driving?"

"Yes, he was. But he's agreed to sit here and wait and not get back in his car."

"Well, that's good," the officer said. "We don't want him to get hurt or to hurt anyone else. But he's not authorized to drive. He's had his license suspended several times."

Raffie looked at the officer and in a friendly plea said, "Is there anything the county or the city or AA can do to help this man? I want to personally help this man."

I could hear the officer sigh again, this time in frustration. "Well, first I have to take him in. Since he was driving and you are a witness, he'll be placed in a cell overnight until first appearances tomorrow morning before the judge. But Raffie, I can pass the judge a note that you want to help Lucas here. Your name goes a long way in this community. The judge also knows you've helped several people before to get back on their feet. But are you willing to do that for Lucas here?"

"Yes, I am willing and able to help him," Raffie quickly asserted. "I can help him in many ways, and hopefully he'll get his life straightened out and be happier."

"But I don't need any help," Lucas suddenly blurted out. "And what about my car?"

Raffie turned to the officer and asked, "Can the car stay here?"

"Well, as long as Miggy is OK with it. And you have to make sure Lucas doesn't come back here and drive again." The officer now turned to the man and said, "Lucas, let me have your car keys."

Lucas struggled to get the keys from the front pocket of his jeans and defiantly handed the officer the keys. The officer gave them to Raffie with a nod. "You must make sure he cannot drive this car until he gets his license back. Raffie, I wouldn't allow this for anyone else but you. The car should really be impounded by the city."

"I can promise you that he will not drive this car," Raffie affirmed to the officer. And then, looking across the street, he added, "I know Diego over there will disable the car. He's got a fenced-in area in the back where he locks up vehicles."

"Disable my car?" the man protested. "What are you going to do?"

Raffie turned to Lucas and said, "Don't worry. It will still run, but just not for you."

The officer asked Lucas to stand up and turn around. Lucas swayed back and forth while the officer attached handcuffs around his wrists.

"I don't want to go back to jail," he snorted. "This is not right."

Raffie said, "I am helping you out, Lucas. Just trust me."

"Right, I'm trusting you, and you git me a ticket to jail."

"It will be better afterward," Raffie assured Lucas in a calm voice. "Just trust me."

The officer walked Lucas to the passenger side of the patrol car. He opened the back door. He gingerly lowered him into the back seat. I watched as the officer placed his hand above the drunk man's head to prevent him from hitting his head on the roof of the patrol car. After closing the car door, the officer walked back up to the porch.

"Raffie, I will send a note to the judge when I get back to the station that you are going to help Lucas." The officer sighed to himself, and shaking his head slightly in disbelief, he said, "I'm amazed you've taken this rehabilitation project on. Hopefully you can help him. No one has been able to do much with him so far. He's habitually in trouble, and no amount of jail time or counseling has helped. I wish you the best of luck."

I watched as the patrol car drove away. Even before the car was out of sight, the old man was already tugging on his pants pocket, pulling out his cell phone.

He turned to me and said, "This is an unusual day for me. Paul, I have to set some things in motion. Bear with me."

I watched as he quickly spun up a call and began speaking into the phone. "Stan, Stan, hey, how are you doing today?"

He listened attentively to the man on the other end of the line and then said, "Well, I have a job for you. It's going to require some work."

The person on the line answered, and I could see the old man nodding his head up and down slowly. "Good. Good. There is a man named Lucas Simpson. He will appear in the city court here tomorrow morning for first appearances. Can you pick him up when the judge decides to release him? He's being booked for driving under the influence with no license. I want you to find a place where we can send him to dry out. I have his car here at Miggy's, and I know Diego will impound it for us."

The old man listened intently to the response and then continued, "That's great. Also get him some new clothes and a haircut and shave. He's ornery, so send one of your best attorneys, one that can deal with him. And also keep me posted."

The old man listened intently again and then said, "Good, good, Stan. I appreciate it. Money is not a big issue here, but try to keep your attorney fees reasonable. I really want this man rehabilitated. I'm going to visit him myself once you have him settled. I'll have some jobs lined up for him as well when he's sober. Oh, also can you find out where he lives and send someone out to his place and see what can be done? Maybe fix the place up a little."

The attorney responded, and Raffie began to smile as he concluded the call. "Thanks, Stan. That's great. I want this man to get back on his feet. I've taken personal responsibility for his recovery."

After the call ended, Raffie did not speak, and he placed his cell phone back in his pants pocket. I watched as he looked out toward the street, and I saw that he had a determined, concerned look on his face. He looked down for a moment and shut his eyes. I was not certain if he was praying or just resting. Afterward he raised his head and opened his eyes. His face seemed to take on an appearance of contentment.

*****

I tilted my head back and took a long, sustained drink from the plastic water bottle. The cool water seemed to revitalize me from the stupor of the afternoon heat. The traffic on the highway was now sporadic, with an occasional eighteen-wheeler racing along the asphalt. The lengthening afternoon shadows continued to creep unremittingly toward the highway.

The old man sat quietly now, staring at the highway. I turned to him, as I wanted to convey an observation that I had made about him. "I can see how you achieved your success. You're resourceful in that you find ways to be successful, making your own way through life's obstacles. And you give back and help others, which is a very admirable quality. I think those traits have made you a success."

The old man showed no impetus to acknowledge my observation, still looking toward the highway. Finally he said, "A success? Maybe."

I responded in disbelief. "If you don't think you're successful, what do you consider success?"

Raffie slowly tilted forward and turned toward me and said, "I believe that most people think success is about money and riches. Money does make your life easier; there is no doubt about that. But it can also create more problems. Problems you never had when you didn't have money. Paul, I believe success is different for different people. Success, I think, is getting to where you want to be, to a place where you have an internal peace and you feel good about yourself, knowing that you worked hard to get to where you are."

I thought for a moment about what he had just said and asked, "How do you know if you can sustain those feelings? Bad things happen that can instantly change your life."

"Yes, life can throw you curveballs. Success does not mean you don't have any problems. Everyone has problems. Life is not static. Everyone ultimately will experience setbacks and tragedies in their lives. For some people, I believe success may be having the peace of mind of just knowing that they conquered and overcame the myriad of problems and tragedies in their lives. Including psychological and mental damage that they may have suffered." The old man stopped and coughed slightly before continuing, "And for some, success may be just learning to avoid the pitfalls of crime or avoiding disastrous relationships or being able to put a lid on an unrelenting addiction. Like for Lucas who was just here. His problems appear to be generational. He needs to break his bad habits and move to a higher level of enjoyment in life. His success, I believe, will be attained when he can shock the world, showing that he can be a productive and stable member of society. I also strongly believe that if he would allow it, he could attain that higher ground through faith. Faith can sustain one through all kinds of setbacks and hardships."

The old man stopped for a moment in thought. I could see a reflective look in his eyes. I thought maybe he was thinking of memories from years ago. Maybe recollections that would bubble up like oil deep in the recesses of his mind, seething upward and expulsed through his words. "Paul, let me tell you a story. I had a friend in 'Nam who was constantly worried about his family's well-being, and it was affecting his mental health. He was very unhappy and always negative about everything going on in his life, and he was quite testy and resentful. Most of the guys felt he was a bad omen—had bad karma, so to speak. They didn't want to patrol with him, and several requested transfers out of our platoon. I was not one of them. One afternoon while our platoon was out on patrol, he stepped on a mine about ten miles from base camp. It took half his leg off. I remember calling for the medic and pressing the artery in his leg to reduce the bleeding. They always told us to do those things if we were in a situation like that. My friend was crying and yelling in pain, and I could see he was going to either die or lose his leg. I felt so bad for him. We had an unspoken kinship." The old man paused and started to wipe the corners of his eyes with the back of his hand. I could see it was difficult for him to unbundle the memories and emotions that were bubbling up from this moment in his past. "The medic came and applied a tourniquet and a dose of ketamine. Twenty minutes later we got him airlifted out by helicopter." He stopped for a moment again, collecting his thoughts, and continued. "Honestly, I would have bet he was going to bleed out and probably not make it. I had seen others do so, and the chances were not very good for him. I know I prayed for him as we continued on the patrol and afterward back at base camp."

Raffie now turned his head toward me and said, "But something miraculous happened that day to my platoon buddy. And I didn't know about it until I got back stateside. George made it back, and they were able to provide him an artificial leg that he could move about on. Later on, I learned from another member of our platoon that George had settled in San Diego. So when I was in San Diego years later, I looked George up and visited him and his family. I was shocked and amazed. George was jovial and in good spirits. He had a real positive attitude on life, which was completely different from how he was in 'Nam. He had joined his brother in business, and the business was doing well. George had a loving wife and two kids. They lived in suburbia and seemed to be very happy. The loss of the leg was a tragedy in his life, but George had overcome it, and I believe he considered his life a success. I know I did."

Raffie stopped to clear his throat and apologized again for his hoarse cough. He continued, "Many years ago, when I was wildcatting, we were doing some exploratory drilling in the Permian Basin down in Texas. There was a man down there, Charlie Dinkins, who owned about fifty scrub acres. Absolutely nothing spectacular about his land. He was scratching out a living and lived in an old, wooden, broken-down three-bedroom home with about six kids. Sad to say, but the locals had humorously nicknamed him 'Good Luck Charlie.' They said if it wasn't for bad luck, Charlie would have no luck at all. I mean, this guy had an old beat-up pickup truck with no tailgate, and the thing looked like it was being held together with Bondo and duct tape. I felt really sorry for him and his family. But they seemed to me to be happy and content. I was hoping we could hit a trap on his property. Several years before, he had allowed some wildcatters to drill on his land, and the wells had come up dry—which was amazing given the amount of oil found in that part of Texas. We were in the area, and I thought maybe we'd take a shot on his land. Maybe the trap was deeper, and with some new technology we dug an exploratory well." Raffie stopped then and started laughing. "Well, Good Luck Charlie Dinkins actually got some good luck. We hit a gusher at twelve to thirteen hundred feet. After that, his fifty acres of scrub produced about five hundred barrels a day for several years. I still remember Charlie running down the hill slapping his cowboy hat against his old dungarees and hollering to his wife and kids, 'We hit oil!' He had oil all over him. He was crazy, hugging his wife and kids, and she was screaming, 'You are ruining our clothes!'"

"I bet that good fortune really changed his life for the better," I said, wishing I had such a fortuitous event in my life. "That's quite a story. He truly became Good Luck Charlie."

The old man slowly shook his head and said, "Paul, it didn't turn out too well for Charlie. He did get a tremendous amount of money in a short time. That ole pickup truck went first. He bought himself a huge dually truck. He built a new eight-bedroom home on the site and tore down the old one. I visited him many times afterward, and gradually things began to happen that brought back the old bad luck, so to speak. After the second year, his wife left him and took the kids to the suburbs of Dallas. She said it was because she now could afford to do so, and she also didn't want to live any longer in such a barren place. Then he took to the bottle too much and got into some drugs and some wild women, and before long he had spent most of the oil money. His health started failing. He had a real bad heart condition."

"Wow, that became a sad story."

"Paul, Charlie was still getting regular oil and gas royalties. He wasn't exactly poor by any stretch, but he was miserable. The last time I saw him before he died, he was down to less than a hundred pounds, and most of his teeth were either missing or dark, and he seemed not to care." The old man looked down at the ground, focusing on a spider that was walking along the edge of the bottom porch rail. I watched his eyes following the spider as he spoke. "You know, Paul, I felt really sorry for Charlie. Thinking back on it, I felt sorrier for him after the oil strike than before. Maybe I did more harm than good."

"That wasn't your fault," I said. "He just wasn't able to handle the changes in his life."

"Maybe so." The old man turned toward me and asked, "So do you think Charlie, with all his money, felt he was successful?"

"No, I would imagine he didn't feel that way," I answered. "It would be hard for him to say he was successful with everything that happened to him. Getting rich was not a good thing for him."

"Exactly, Paul. Charlie must have felt that he gained the world but lost everything he loved and cherished. In my opinion, in his situation, only through faith could he have truly felt peace."

*****

It was now past three o'clock, and the heat was building toward its final peak for the day. I continued drinking from the large bottle of water, trying to stay hydrated. The water was no longer cool, but it was still refreshing.

Out of the corner of my eye, I spotted what looked like a dog up the highway looking toward us. It was standing still and staring at the porch. It was a medium-height dog, and the fur was long and thick. I noticed a trace of light color underneath it, and it had a bushy, black-tipped tail.

I turned to Raffie and pointed at the animal and inquired, "I wonder whose dog that is. It must be lost. Hopefully someone didn't abandon it."

The old man turned to look where I was pointing. He squinted his eyes and then chuckled, saying, "That's nobody's dog—that's a wild coyote. We see quite a few coyotes around here. But you don't normally see very many in the daytime."

I looked again at the animal up the road and said, "It looks like a miniature wolf. Do they attack people?"

"Not generally. They like small animals, and sometimes they'll bring down a bigger animal if it's sick or weak or they have some help. But it's very unlikely they would attack you. He'll run along in a minute."

Minutes later I heard a familiar ring from the old man's cell phone. He slowly pulled the phone from his pants pocket and turned to me and said, "I apologize, Paul. I have to get this call."

I watched again as his aged and gnarled fingers attempted to locate the touch screen button to connect the call.

"Hello, Meghan. Since you are calling back so soon, you must have some good news for me?"

I watched as the old man listened intently, pressing the phone tight against his ear. "Well, well. Let's hold firm and wait on this deal. The fact they countered so quickly means they really want the property. We can be patient and let them come to our price."

I looked at Raffie's bronzed face. His eyes were squinting underneath his thick, unkempt eyebrows as he once again assumed his businesslike countenance.

"Good. Meghan, we know this property is a gem. There's nothing like it in that area. It's a great retail location. If they want it, they have to meet our number. I'm not in any hurry to sell. We still have quite a few opportunities out there in the Florida, Arizona, and Texas markets. Things are starting to move."

The old man once again listened and then responded, "It's good to know that retail commercial property is moving quicker in that area as well. And if this company truly needs a premier location, as they have said, we have a great property for them."

He kept looking down at the floor of the porch as he spoke into the phone. "Well, I saw the latest pictures you sent me of the site. Not much they need to do to the land to begin building on it. I'm sure they'll come around. And if this deal gets done, let's maybe look at acquiring something in the Flagstaff area. I'm reading and hearing some good things are happening in that market. People are retiring and moving south, and developers are hungry for land."

He listened again and then said, "Great! Well, you have a great rest of the day also, and take care. I appreciate your hard work on this. Keep me informed. Bye, Meghan."

He slowly placed the cell phone back in his front pants pocket. "I'm sorry, Paul, for the phone interruption," he said apologetically. "It's still a thrill to work on a deal. I like to think it keeps me young and helps my mind to stay active."

I smiled. I knew that feeling also. It always felt great when I could bring a deal to the table and close a large commercial loan. It was a tremendous feeling of accomplishment. The feeling I think is probably primordial, like that of hunting and bringing down a large prey animal by yourself and triumphantly carrying it back through your village.

I asked cautiously, "Raffie, not trying to get into your business, but just curious—why did you start buying and selling real estate?"

He exhaled slowly, and I could sense a little hesitation in his voice as he responded. "I...I...I usually don't discuss my business dealings. But, uh, as you can imagine, I was receiving revenue for many years from my oil business and needed to find something to invest in. Thirty years ago, I purchased my first commercial property in Houston and sold it three months later for a sizable profit. So from there I started working with commercial and retail property realtors all over Texas, looking for choice property to acquire. And then, after vacationing in Florida one year, I started looking for commercial property sites there. I would ask the realtors to find properties in parts of the outskirts of major cities where expansion was likely to occur and the property taxes were lower. And because I was not in any hurry to sell the property, it just sat there and appreciated each year. I have sufficient cash flow and more than enough to live on. In reality, I am fortunate to have had the opportunity to work with some great realtors. They directed me where I needed to cast my net out, as they knew where there would be plenty of fish in the future to harvest. Years on, now it's just a matter of pulling in the net and reaping the harvest."

I asked, "It sounds like you own quite a lot? I mean, you've got land in Texas and Florida."

The old man smiled. "Well. I suppose you could say I have a lot."

"You bought all your properties sight unseen?" I asked.

"No, I always visit a potential purchase site before I make an offer. But I don't look to acquire anything that is less than twenty acres or is not a well-maintained prime commercial building."

"Did you ever turn down anything a realtor suggested?"

"Oh yes, I have. When we started looking at properties in Arizona and Colorado, I had to get a lot more selective. I didn't know much about acquiring property initially in those places. So I was really careful and turned down quite a few deals."

As a banker, I know sometimes the commercial real estate market is good, and sometimes it's not so good, so I asked, "Holding the property long term, you probably didn't get hurt too much with the downturns in the real estate market?"

"Yes. Everything has a cycle. If you don't have to sell, you just hold. If the market is way down, you buy, buy, buy. When the market recovers, you sell. So far, I have been very blessed to be able to be patient and buy and sell when it made sense to do so."

"Well, if you can do it, that's a great strategy," I said. "A few of my clients have gotten stuck in the downturns. They had to sell their property in distressed sales to pay off their loans." I grimaced as I admitted, "Unfortunately some of my clients had to take losses, and the bank had to absorb some write-offs."

*****

Raffie was rubbing the gray bristles on his chin when a motorcycle pulled up to the steps. I watched as a slender young man in his twenties climbed off the cycle and took his helmet off. He was dark complected, and his short black hair was groomed closely to each side of his clean-shaven face. He broke into a smile immediately upon seeing Raffie.

"You are just the person I'm looking for," he said excitedly, bounding up the steps.

The old man looked up smiling and calmly said, "Alphonso, good to see you. How are you doing today?"

"Doing great now!" he exclaimed excitedly. The young man spoke loudly, trying to contain his excitement. His words shot out like a geyser full of force that couldn't be stopped. "I got the job at Hutchinson's Tractor Company that we talked about."

In his unbridled joy, the young man reached out and shook the old man's hand vigorously. I was concerned his aggressive hand shaking was going to hurt Raffie's arm and shoulder. The exuberant young man continued, "I know you help so many people, and I knew that coming to you for advice would be good. And I know you put a good word in for me, and I appreciate that. The opportunity they are giving me is great. I can't thank you enough,

Mr. Raffie. I never could have gotten this job without your help."

Raffie studied the young man for a moment as he stood there moving back and forth and still smiling broadly with excitement. He asked in a calm tone, "Alphonso, did you tell them that you had worked at Harper's farm since you were seventeen? And also that you had been going to school at night, taking business courses?"

"Yes sir, just as you said," he answered, nodding profusely. The young man now stood in front of Raffie, standing erect with his chest out, displaying a passionate self-pride. He continued, "And I also looked him in the eye during the interview and shook his hand before and after the interview like you said. I did everything you told me to do."

Raffie leaned back in his chair now and smiled. His voice suddenly took on a celebratory tone. "Well, Alphonso, you did good! I am so very happy for you! I had heard you were a real good worker and that you were very ambitious."

"Yes, sir," he said. "And I appreciate again everything you did for me, telling Hutchinson about me and all. Oh, I did tell him, as you told me, that if he gave me a chance, I would work very hard, and he wouldn't be disappointed. And Mr. Raffie, that is true. I will work very hard and try to be the best salesperson they have. I don't want to hurt your reputation since you recommended me."

"Well, Alphonso, again, I'm happy for you. You did well, and now it's time that you and your family should celebrate this occasion. Are you going to celebrate tonight?"

The young man laughed, throwing his head backward, and answered, "Yes, I'm going inside to buy some beer and wine and some party food. Lucia is going to cook, and we are going to have a big party tonight. Our family and some of our neighbors are coming over to celebrate. You are welcome to join us."

The old man chuckled to himself. "Alphonso, thank you for asking, but I don't get out much anymore at night. I'm too old now, and I'm in bed by nine anyway. But enjoy this occasion with your family and friends."

"Well, Mr. Raffie, if you change your mind, feel free to stop by. You know where we live. We'd love to have you over. But I guess I better go inside now and get everything Lucia wants me to pick up for tonight."

The young man turned and opened the screen door and bounded inside like a jackrabbit. I could hear him enthusiastically telling Miggy about his new job. After a few minutes, he returned through the screen door.

He stopped on the front porch and said to the old man, "Thank you again, Mr. Raffie. I wouldn't have gotten the job without your advice."

Raffie nodded and said, "But Alphonso, you got the job on your own. You had to sell yourself. The folks at Hutchinson's didn't interview me for the job."

The young man in an appreciative tone continued, "Yes, but you put a good word in for me. You know they don't always hire people that look like me. You know what I mean. I am not like their other sales managers."

The young man turned and descended the steps to his motorcycle. He carefully picked up his helmet and put it on his head and placed the groceries in the side compartment.

The old man leaned forward and said, "Alphonso, you should know one thing."

"What is that?" he asked as he climbed onto his motorcycle.

"I did not speak to anyone at Hutchinson's. You got the job entirely on your interview."

The young man paused, taking in the old man's words. Then he slowly responded in bewilderment that turned into excitement, "Really? Really? Wow!"

*****

I knew my car would be ready in less than an hour now. I looked across the street, and I could see the car was parked inside one of the bays. The hood was down, and Diego was working inside the car. I started figuring out my time schedule for the evening. I needed to get to my flight at eight twenty. If I left just before four thirty, I should be at the airport in Albuquerque just before eight. If I had the time, I could stop and fill the gas tank on the way to the airport. If not, I'd let them charge my corporate card to top the gas tank off. Then, since I had only a carry-on bag, I figured it would take less than fifteen minutes to get through security and walk through the terminal to my departure gate. The only concern I had was that when I got to the rental car office, I needed to give them the paid repair invoice. Hopefully that wouldn't take too much time. The rental-car company had agreed to reimburse me for the repair work when I called them early that morning. If all worked out, I should be at my gate no later than eight fifteen, with five minutes to spare. It seemed tight, but I'd done it many times before. In a way it was quite exhilarating to race against the clock.

*****

The old man slowly stirred and turned to me and asked, "Paul, you know something you should never say?"

I smiled and responded, "I can think of many things I should never say."

The old man laughed and said, "I guess I need to be more specific. But you should never say *never*. Sometimes things just happen in your life that change your perspective on things."

"That's for sure," I said. "*Never* is never an absolute."

"Paul, when I got back from 'Nam, I never wanted to hold or shoot a gun again. But about forty years ago, someone broke into our house and stole my wife's jewelry and some collectibles I had." He paused, shaking his head in disbelief. "You know, it made me so mad that someone could do that. And they did it while we were out of town. You feel so violated, like someone literally has invaded your life. Marcia and I felt so vulnerable for a long time afterward."

As I listened to Raffie, I thought that I was fortunate in that I had never experienced a home robbery. However, there had been one night when I was in college that my roommate forgot to lock the door to our dorm room, and someone had come in during the night and stolen our schoolbooks. I did remember the feeling of being a little scared afterward. And I did feel violated and helpless.

"Paul, the people that burglarized our home were never caught. Marcia was so frightened after that, thinking they might return. I felt I had to do something to make her feel safe and protect our family. So I bought a rifle and a handgun. They are fully licensed, and I keep both weapons clean and in a locked cabinet in the house. I did find some other uses also for firearms. I bought a twenty-gauge shotgun and took up skeet and trap shooting. And I got good at it. It was fun. Have you ever been skeet shooting?"

I shook my head. "No, I haven't ever shot a gun. I've always been afraid to own anything like that with kids in the house. You hear all those horror stories of kids getting accidentally shot and all. But I personally don't have a problem if someone has a firearm and they use it responsibly for hunting or for safety."

The old man continued, "Paul, having that feeling of helplessness and being a crime victim changed my perspective on lawful guns. I hear people in the cities want to take everyone's guns away. But in a free country, you'd never be able to take them away from the bad guys out there. They'd find a way to buy guns and commit crimes." He sighed to himself and then continued in a thoughtful tone, "The only saving grace with trying to take guns from everybody is it would be harder for the true crazy people out there to get guns."

I nodded my head slowly in agreement. "It does seem like there are a lot of crazy people out there today that have access to guns."

"Paul, our society needs to find a way to keep crazy people from having guns. In the old days, they had public mental institutions where the criminally insane would be put to protect themselves and society. Honestly, it's sad to say, but some of those asylums were doing horrific things to those mentally insane individuals. Using them for experiments and such. And some folks were institutionalized that should not have been. As a result, a lot of states dismantled and downsized their mental institutions."

"Maybe we should revisit the asylum approach again?" I wondered out loud. "At least get the really dangerous folks off the street. Maybe that would prevent some of the senseless mass shootings."

"That would require some political will that I don't think exists at this time," Raffie said.

I agreed with Raffie's last point, and I said, "Personally, I don't see any issue with taking mentally ill people who are dangerous off the streets. I mean, if a close family member requests their kin be institutionalized for public safety, I'm fine with that. A medical professional would still need to do an evaluation before someone would be committed. I would think that would need to be a minimum requirement." I stopped and thought about it further and added, "Or if law enforcement and a professional mental health worker identified someone as criminally insane and dangerous to society, I think that person should be institutionalized as well."

"I don't know what the answer is here," the old man said, rubbing his chin. "But we need something done, and it needs to be different from how it is today and better than it used to be."

I started thinking more about this issue and thoughtfully added, "Maybe to avoid the abuses, the institutions could be closely monitored and regulated by each state. Maybe there could be some kind of commonsense federal and state laws on how the people in these institutions should be treated. You know, like guidelines in a nursing home. And maybe the state or federal government could do periodic well-being and checkup audits on the institutions. Have a whistleblower program for abuses also, or something like that."

"That might work," the old man answered. "There has to be a better solution, and maybe preemptively institutionalizing the criminally insane to protect society is the only answer."

"If that was done, and it did prevent some of the horrific mass shootings in our society today, it would be worth trying again," I said. "Also, maybe make the punishment more severe if a gun was used to commit a crime."

The old man slowly turned toward me to make a point. "Paul, believe it or not, we have fewer people per capita being murdered today than in the olden days."

"Yeah, I guess we don't have vigilantes running around anymore like in the frontier days. And there aren't any crazy bounty hunters, Wild West outlaw gangs, or pistol duels today."

"We do still have gangs," the old man quipped. "They just don't ride on horses."

I started to think about the safety of my family. How would I protect my family if someone broke into our house at night? Should I purchase a gun? Was I foolish not to be ready if such an event were to occur?

I thought I needed to make another point on this issue. "Raffie, I think today we also glorify violence too much in our society. It has made everyone somewhat desensitized to violence. In our home, my wife and I have restricted our kids from playing violent video games. We also have restricted the television and movies they watch. But it's hard, because you can see violence played out everywhere on television and in the movies. And you know, not every parent is as responsible as we try to be." I paused and sighed. "It's impossible to shut it out completely."

The old man slowly nodded his head and answered, "Violence and guns today are a pervasive problem in our society. I don't think the forefathers could have predicted all the senseless shootings we have in some of our cities. But given all that, there is a reason we have the Second Amendment."

"Just why did they put that in the Constitution? Other than for hunting and protecting our families, do we really need guns to be protected by the Constitution?"

Raffie slowly leaned back in his chair and answered, "The Second Amendment is meant to protect the citizens from an authoritarian tyrannical government—like it was in England with the king. The citizenry had no way to protect themselves or defend themselves against a corrupt despot."

"But is that realistic today?" I asked. "We're a democracy, and I don't see how a single party despot could take control and take our rights away."

"Maybe so or maybe not. We've never gotten to that point. But look at Nazi Germany. It took less than five years for Germany to move from a democratic republic to an authoritarian dictatorship. It can happen."

"I understand that. And we don't want to be like the old Soviet Union or North Korea or Communist China either."

The old man slowly nodded in agreement. "But for the protection of society, going back to our discussion, we do need to identify those who are mentally dangerous and insane. They should never get access to firearms." The old man paused and added, thinking out loud, "But I still have a problem with some of the weapons that are available for sale. I don't know if I agree with having powerful assault weapons in the hands of everyone. At least not without ensuring they are lawful owners and the firearms are kept secured. I do agree the states should run background checks initially and periodically on the holders of these weapons. I know that option is not popular with everyone today."

*****

The screen door opened, and Miggy popped his head out. "You gentlemen need anything more to drink or eat?" I turned toward the screen door and saw Miggy smiling at the both of us. Miggy seemed like a real likable guy. He had a friendly, round face that seemed to have a constant pleasant look permanently planted on it. It was easy to understand why these two men had bonded as friends.

The old man looked down at his watch and then turned toward the screen door and said, "Mig, in about a half hour, you can bring us a couple of more sandwiches." He then looked at me and asked, "Paul, will that work with your schedule?"

"That will work," I answered. "But Mig, if it's not too much trouble, could I get another bottle of water?"

"No problem," Miggy answered.

Raffie slowly got up from his chair. I watched him as he used the armrests to push himself upward. I could hear the joints in his knees crack as he slowly turned, moving forward with mini steps. As he walked to the screen door, he braced himself, holding on to the arm of the chair for support.

"You'll have to excuse me," he said. "I have to use the bathroom."

"No problem," I answered, smiling. "I'm not going to stop you."

The old man chuckled to himself. "Well, good. I'll be back."

The old man slowly opened the screen door and disappeared inside. As there was no wind blowing at the moment, I could feel the heaviness of the heat emanating from the parking lot. I looked across the street. Diego was working again on my rental car. I was thinking how great it would be to get back home, where at least it was a bit more comfortable outside. And the next weekend at my dad's house would be even more comfortable. My dad lives by a large lake up in the Cascades. It's always a fun time for the kids up there, as there are plenty of things to do outside. My dad always makes our time with him as pleasurable as possible. I think missing my mother and being by himself, he is really lonely and enjoys our visits.

*****

All day long, cars and trucks had pulled up to Miggy's, and the occupants had gone inside and exited with things to drink and grocery bags full of meats and vegetables and canned goods. Miggy had a large clientele and a good location. Most of his customers seemed to be regulars, and the abundant traffic was constant. When I looked up and down the street, there were only a few buildings in sight. And I saw no other grocery stores or restaurants where one could stop for refreshments or food. I easily understood why he was so busy.

Miggy came outside again and handed me a cold bottle of water. I could feel the coldness seeping into my hands as I grasped the bottle. "Here you go," he said. "Raffie will take care of it."

I looked up and said, "Thanks. I really don't expect him to pay for this."

Miggy responded, "He doesn't care. He likes to have people he can talk to. In a way you are making the day pass quicker for him. On some days he sits out here for hours by himself. It's good that you are here today to provide him company."

I lifted the bottle slowly to my mouth and took a drink. I watched the condensation running down the sides of the bottle. I don't recall water ever tasting as good.

After a short time, the screen door opened, and the old man came slowly out, carefully shutting the door behind him. He walked by me and, reversing his movements, descended back into the chair. I could hear the chair make a creaking sound as he comfortably positioned himself.

He looked at me and said, "Good, you got water."

"Raffie, I feel like I owe you something for the food and drink today. It's nice of you, but I'm not expecting you to pay for everything."

The old man smiled. "That's exactly why I don't mind. You don't expect it. If you expected it, I might have some second thoughts."

"Well, I still feel guilty not paying for everything. It's awfully nice of you."

The old man seemed settled in his chair now and began again, "My son and daughter don't visit as much as they used to. My grandkids are older now and are beginning to have lives of their own. I get cards from them thanking me for gifts and such, but few visits." There was a melancholy tone in his voice.

"Paul, I can still take care of myself," he continued. "My daughter checks in on me every week, usually by phone, to ask me how I'm doing. Having a caring daughter is a great thing, you know. And my son also does call me every once in a while. But not as frequently as my daughter."

"Does your daughter live nearby?" I asked.

"No, she's in Chicago. She and her husband own a business, and they do pretty good with it. They're busy all the time." He paused and seemed to reflect on his last statement and continued, "You know, I was busy all the time when I was working, and there were some times I was away from home for weeks at a time. I do regret not being around my son and daughter more when they were younger. And when I think back on it, I was like my dad. I didn't see him as much as the other kids in our neighborhood saw their dads. And now it's come full circle, and my kids don't have any time to spend with me. They are too busy with their work and families. And I fully understand all that."

He added in a pensive, reflective tone, "Our kids were great kids. They may have had an absent father for stretches, but they had a great mother. Marcia was good at raising them and teaching them the difference between right and wrong." He looked down at the porch deck, searching for the right words. "As I said, everyone has some regrets in their life. I wish I had been home more when they were little. I was never around to see when they first rolled over as babies or began to take their first steps. I wasn't there for their first days of school, and I missed out on all their school events. But I can't turn back time. The irony is that today I have more time than I need. But the past is the past. It's now carved in stone. I can only try to make up today for the many years I was away from home." He stopped and looked up into the sky. "Paul, you have to live your life as it comes to you sometimes. In the midst of life, you can't always discern the other side of the coin. It's not till later that you realize what you missed and can't get back. Time is so precious, so enjoy every moment you can with your family."

The old man stopped and cleared his throat. "Paul, as I perceive my time on this earth, it seems to be moving quicker as I get older. I know that doesn't seem possible. One would think that with less going on as you get older, time would be slower. But when I was younger and busier, I could mark time by so many more events in my life. And I didn't have the perspective of time passage that I do today. But as you retire and grow older, there are fewer events that mark your time. There are a lot more old memories and fewer new memories. Your days may seem slower as you live them, but when you think backward, time appears to have speeded up. I believe fewer activities equate to a faster passage of time. When I think about something that happened recently, I'm always shocked to find out it actually happened five years ago or maybe ten years ago. It makes you think more about how time passes so quickly. And my day today won't be a whole lot different from tomorrow or the next day as I continue my life journey. But when I think back on the many memories I have, it does seem like it took a long time to get here."

I nodded and said, "You know, there are times I wish my time would speed up. Sometimes I can't wait to retire and have more free time. And have my mind completely free of worries and stress."

The old man turned to me and chuckled. "Paul, just be careful what you ask for. It's good to have a few worries in your life. Some stress in your life is not bad."

I watched the old man as he adjusted himself in the chair, wigglingx his back to get comfortable. "In my life, like everybody's life, there have been good times and not-so-good times. When I say not-so-good times, I'm not talking about personal tragedies, like when I lost my parents and Marcia. And I've had my share of tragedies. You never forget those. But when I look back on the other periods in my life, none of the not-so-good times seem to be as bad as I thought at the time. It all seems to run together in my memory, and everything is just grouped as the past. And in the past, the grudges and disagreements and unfortunate events in life fade and don't seem to matter as much anymore."

"I can see that," I responded. "I've worked with people or in jobs I didn't necessarily like. When I think back on those experiences, they don't seem so bad now."

*****

I looked up to see two dusty and faded pickup trucks pulling into the parking lot. As the trucks came to a stop, a large cloud of dust descended upon the porch. Almost instantly the front doors of the two trucks opened simultaneously, as if they were choreographed. Each door made a discordant metal noise, as if they both had been stuck and needed to be pried open. Several young men climbed out, some without shirts, some wearing bandanas on their heads, and all wearing faded work jeans. I would guess that not one of them was beyond his mid-twenties.

I watched the old man looking at the young men as they passed us entering the grocery. Several nodded and acknowledged our presence as they sauntered by us. Their shoes scraped along the wooden floor of the porch like sandpaper. Some strode by us slowly with their heads up, and others just trotted forward, looking down as they passed. One of the men who passed was wearing a faded ball cap with "USS Newport News" printed on it. Once they were inside, I could hear them talking and clamoring over what they wanted to eat and drink. Some spoke Spanish as they made their choices. After a while the young men came out one by one and were standing by their pickup trucks. I watched as they popped the tops of their beer cans and consumed their sandwiches and chips. The sandwiches were wrapped in white paper that glistened in the late-afternoon sun. I thought their workday was done and maybe this was an everyday ritual for them. It seemed like a post-work communion.

I watched as they mingled and embraced their fellowship of life. I wondered, what will these young men do later in life when the hot sun and labor are too much for them?

Is there a step up to a next level of existence and survival for them? Do they become foremen and work less in the field when they get older? But how many foreman jobs are there? The young men seemed happy and were laughing and occasionally punching each other in the arm. When something humorous was said, it would trigger laughter from the entire group of men. I could hear a few speaking English as they cajoled each other.

Raffie appeared to be amused watching the men, and turning to me he said, "As I said earlier, these young men keep everything going in this country. They are the workers that we rely on every day, but no one sees them. Most people look right through them and don't want to see them. But these folks are some of us. They battle with struggles, and they fight each day to scratch out a living." The old man stopped for a second. "They are not hollow, transparent people. They must be seen and heard. They all have stories to tell, but few would care to listen. What's sad is the most prominent among us are afraid of these types of young men and women. They keep their distance from them. And why?"

I answered, "I guess people think that they might be criminals or something? Or they can't relate to them?"

"The elite are afraid because they are dependent on these folks," said the old man. "They have prejudged and labeled them based on their jobs, education, and lifestyles. They are seen as the bottom level of society. But they are not. They are called rednecks and roughnecks and other derogative monikers, but they are completely misunderstood. They have dreams, aspirations, and desires like everyone else. They want the freedom to chase their dreams and fulfill their full potential. We must acknowledge as a country that we cannot marginalize or limit them."

I nodded, understanding. "They haven't been given much respect."

"Yes, we can respect them by providing better opportunities," the old man responded. "First, we need to make sure they have jobs and can make a living. If they are unemployed, their well-being and self-respect are destroyed. Without jobs, there is no future. And also, importantly, we must help them make good decisions. For example, we need to show them how to invest for the future, how to go back to school if they have the ability to do so, how to work to achieve a successful marriage, how to get a new job, or how to start a new business. There are programs like this already, but they don't reach everybody. We have to help them move into a middle-class lifestyle. The jobs they are doing are important, but they cannot work outdoors in the sun here forever. As they get older, their stamina will decrease. Their wives, sisters, and mothers also need help in making the right decisions. Not a handout but help up. I am a strong believer that being dependent on the government for everything is wrong. Society will see these young workers as a drag on our country if they are only supported by our government. The government can help, but it cannot be the total solution."

The old man stopped and looked up again at the men standing in the parking lot. "It is important that community charities also assist those who are really in need. The American spirit is to give. Both the wealthy and not so wealthy should freely give to charities or at least volunteer to help worthwhile causes. And I'm talking about rolling up your sleeves, not for show or as a publicity stunt but honestly working to improve people's lives. We should continue to encourage that behavior. These workers are not victims. There have always been less fortunate people since the dawn of mankind. There always will be. People built the pyramids in the heat of the Egyptian desert, and people slaved in the jungles of South America, and others scratched out a living in Southeast Asia and Africa. There have been countless periods of misery due to wars and oppressive despots. The Roman and Greek slaves toiled under terrible working conditions. Do their descendants feel like they are victims today? Abuse and atrocities were everywhere in the Old World. Again, there always will be less fortunate people among us. But we need to help them make the right decisions, and we need to respect these folks. I believe that from those to whom much has been given, much is expected. We all can do more. But making them societal victims or wards of the state only makes their self-esteem and lives worse. And that can ultimately lead to resentment by others as well in our society."

I thought for a moment about my father's situation as a young man. My father's mom died when he was ten years old. His father passed away when he was sixteen. In essence, he was an orphan at sixteen in high school. His uncle and aunt took him in and encouraged him to join the service. He enlisted in the navy and was able to learn a trade. He told me he'd always liked tinkering with things, and he found his calling working on airplanes. That experience in the navy improved his self-confidence and gave him a sense of pride. Later on, that experience allowed him to make a reasonable living working for an airline. I thought that as a young man he probably had no idea where his life would lead him. He could have gone down a different path, and his life could have been much more difficult. It worked out with a hand up, fortunately for me.

The young men in the sandy parking lot continued their social frivolity and bantering back and forth. The old man sat back in his chair and sighed, "To be young again." He chuckled to himself. "If I could only have been more mature as a young man, how much more could I do today to help people?"

"But would it have been as much fun growing up?" I asked.

"Probably not. Probably not," he confessed. "Paul, in those young men, I see a unity of spirit. Just look at them. There are probably three or four different racial groups comingling, and they are getting along fine. This is the American spirit that we need to show the world. This is what can be done."

I nodded in agreement. "We are, I guess, somewhat unique in the world in that we have so many different ethnic and cultural groups living together. There are a few countries like us, but not many."

The old man turned and said, "If we succeed, it will be a great leap forward for the rest of the planet. I just hope the politicians don't muck it up. When you force people to accept things or, worse, deceive the populace by clouding the truth, things ultimately get mucked up. People resent being deceived. They also resent losing their identity, pride, and heritage. It's like we have to make mashed potatoes with a fork."

I wasn't sure I followed exactly the analogy he was using, but I nodded. "There will always be some lumps, I suppose."

"We have a war today going on between two important parts of our lives. Which take precedence—family values or societal values? Both are equally important in maintaining a unified country where each citizen is respected and we have some semblance of harmony. In my culture, family is always first, and community and society are second. But in some cultures, conformity to societal norms is first. It's really tough to blend the different cultures. And when you try to change culture or heritage, you run up against people not assimilating or accepting our country's values."

"So how do you blend everybody together?" I asked. "Especially when some resist change?"

The old man looked up again at the young men as they began piling back into their work trucks. "You can't force anyone to do anything they don't want to do, unless you threaten them with some form of violence or punishment. There are plenty of examples of that today and in the past. The last things we need are reeducation camps or government indoctrination programs."

"So how do you blend everybody together?" I asked again.

"Paul, sad to say, I don't think it can be done quickly. It will take time. On an individual basis, most people will always accept and respect one another based on character and personality. However, there are still differences in culture and ethnic groups and heritage that separate us." He sighed and looked across the street for a moment and continued, "We live in a strange society here in America. We ask diverse people with different cultures, heritages, religions, and ethnicities to work together for the good. Which is a good thing. However, we also have a system that requires each of us to compete against others. Competition leads to winners and losers, and no one wants to be a loser. The losers in any group will complain they are treated unfairly, right or wrong. And this applies to everyone."

I was thinking about Raffie's words as I studied the wooden deck railing. I had noticed all afternoon the faded red paint chipping from the railing. The railing probably had not been painted in twenty years. I could see at the base of each spindle the mounting growth of dry wood rot. Back home in Seattle, with our rainfall, this railing would have collapsed years ago.

"Raffie, as a country we do have a challenge, don't we?"

"I know this is a difficult issue to discuss today," Raffie slowly answered. "How do we assimilate everyone into our American culture? How do we keep the American Dream alive?" He stopped for a moment and seemed to be contemplating his next words. "We need to ensure that everyone has an equal opportunity to achieve success. We cannot and should not guarantee equal outcomes. As we work to achieve equal opportunities for all, our society and culture will need to change. The question is, will our American values, economic system, and culture change to the point that we no longer have the values that made America exceptional? That made America unique and great?"

I nodded in agreement. "That is a good question. Will we change too much? Can we change without losing our identity?"

"As our society changes," the old man continued, "there is another problem that I worry about today. When I was growing up, we were expected to go to the cathedral for worship once a week. Sometimes more often. Did it make us good people? No, not everyone. But you knew the world was not just about you. There was a higher power. I worry today that some young people are shunning any religion or moral teaching. It's a trend in our society, and I truly worry about these young people. Will they have difficulties coping when life becomes extremely difficult, as it always does? Will we see more drug and alcohol abusers? Will crime go up? Will there be more domestic violence? More hate crimes? What will the future look like?"

Not being a very religious person, I did wonder about that myself. Would laws have to be stricter in the future and punishments more severe? Would some individual rights need to be curtailed to ensure the safety and well-being of our society? Would we have more mass shootings? Would our streets be unsafe? I knew that moral teachings could not be institutionalized. And I knew that moral teachings had to be reinforced at home and exemplified at home.

But as stress was placed on families, would they be able to reinforce and exemplify the right moral behaviors?

"Paul, we live on this rocky planet swirling in space in a small, infinitesimal part of a massive, unbelievable universe. Maybe there are even more universes out there. Is it all by accident and chance? And are we to live and die, never knowing or understanding why?"

"That's the age-old question," I said. "Is there a purpose in our existence?" This was beginning to be quite a broadening discussion on life. I thought to myself in amusement, *how did we get from talking about the passage of time and then about American culture and society and then religious moral teaching to now pondering our understanding of the universe?* I wondered where the old man would take this conversation next.

Raffie's dark eyes suddenly narrowed as he looked up into the sky. As he spoke, his brow was furrowed, and his face displayed a deeply concerned look that I thought to be quite intense.

"Paul, mankind has existed on this planet for just a short time. Yet we are the only living things that can destroy all of it. Why are we able to do this? Why have we been given consciousness? Why can we perceive reality? Why has such free will been given to us that we are capable of doing great things, and yet also capable of being so destructive and evil? For me, I accept that there is simply a higher power.

Somehow in all this there is a plan. To me it seems so, so it must be so. But I don't force my beliefs on others. They can believe what they wish."

At that moment a loud screeching sound filled the air, followed by a bang of metal crashing together. Instinctively I looked up to see the source of the calamity. Just a few hundred feet down the highway were two cars fused together, with what appeared to be steam rising above one of the vehicles. Several vehicles behind the accident were pulling off to the side of the road. A few seconds later, a tall middle-aged man ran to the collided cars and, along with a short elderly man, began helping the occupants out of their cars. One gray-haired woman in a blue dress was holding a cell phone to her ear. I assumed she was calling the police to report the accident. Several people gathered around the two cars and were talking to the occupants.

A man who had been removed from one of the cars kept rubbing his head with a handkerchief and looking down at it. His white shirt, even at this distance, appeared to have bright red blotches along the button line. One of the spectators took this man by the arm and walked him across the street. She held the man's left arm and shoulder, helping him to sit down under the shade of a large plumbing-supply billboard. The occupants in the other car had gotten out on their own. They appeared to be young adults, maybe teenagers. It didn't seem from our distance that they had sustained any injuries. One of the occupants, a young girl, appeared to be crying, wiping tears periodically from her face. The two young boys with her were on their cell phones. As they spoke on their phones, they turned their heads away from the collided vehicles from time to time, looking toward the porch. They appeared from this distance to be quite emotional.

"That happened quickly," I said, pointing to the man sitting in the shade. "I hope he's OK over there on the curb." I watched numerous people trying to assist him as he sat in the shade. The injured man was holding the handkerchief against his forehead and was tilting his head backward, I assumed to slow the bleeding.

"Paul, accidents seem to happen along this highway too often. I've seen at least four in the last two years. From here, thank God, it does look like no one was seriously hurt. Hopefully a medic gets here soon to help that man."

I was looking at the cars crumpled together, and I was trying to figure out how the collusion had occurred. The car in front had been rear-ended at an angle from the right side. The young driver who had been driving behind the first car must have tried to avoid the collision. I thought probably the first car had slowed or stopped for some reason. The second car must have braked and tried to swerve off the road but skidded sideways into the first car from behind.

I could see a glistening of water or gasoline building on the highway. A middle-aged man in a white shirt was trying to corral the spectators away from the accident. He had his arms in the air and was frantically motioning everyone to get away from the collided cars and move off the road.

The traffic was beginning to back up, as the accident had blocked the highway in both directions. The spectators had formed an opening on the right side of the highway to allow a few cars near the front of the line to pull through an adjacent field to navigate around the blockage.

An elderly couple who had left their car stood in the middle of the highway, gawking at the two mangled vehicles. The elderly man was shaking his head in disbelief. The injured driver remained seated in the shade and sat motionless, still pressing the handkerchief against his forehead. I watched as a middle-aged woman in jeans came out from the plumbing-supply store. She gave the man a bottle of water and some paper towels. He began to drink the water, and he poured some of the water onto a paper towel, slowly dabbing at his forehead.

I began wondering how long it would take the police to get there. I figured a fire truck would come as well, since there might be gasoline on the road. I did not hear any sirens yet.

Miggy had come out the screen door to investigate the cause of the noise. "I heard the collision," he said, looking up the highway at the accident. "Is everyone OK?"

"Yes, I think so," I answered, and I pointed to the injured man sitting on the curb. "The man over there by the plumbing store had blood coming from his head, but I don't think it's too serious. He's talking to everyone and seems OK."

"That's good," Miggy replied. "You know, we get a lot of accidents around here for some reason. I don't know why. It's a straight highway here, and there aren't any blind curves or hidden side streets. The police will be along here shortly. They usually clean these accidents up quickly. The highway can't be blocked for long."

The old man adjusted himself in his chair and, shaking his head, echoed Miggy. "I just don't understand either why we have so many accidents along this highway. It doesn't make any sense."

Miggy seemed satisfied that no one needed assistance, and he turned and went back inside, muttering to himself, "Hopefully the police will get here quickly."

"I bet the folks in the accident would like to have their day as a do-over," said Raffie. "A mulligan."

I nodded and said sympathetically, "You know, accidents are bad for everyone involved. It doesn't matter whether you are at fault or not. Auto accidents are just inconveniences. You have to deal with insurance companies and repair shops. And while your car is being repaired, sometimes you have to be provided another vehicle just to get around. I do feel sorry for the folks involved."

In the distance, I could now hear the faint wailing of sirens. It had been about five minutes since the accident. The siren sounds grew louder as the emergency vehicles got closer. One of the sirens had an alternating sound, making an annoying shrill noise even from a distance.

As the emergency vehicles approached, I looked up the road and could see cars pulling off to the side of the road to allow the first responders to proceed toward the accident. Then more and more cars began pulling off the road. Then I saw a police car moving swiftly through the gauntlet of vehicles. A fire rescue truck was not far behind. The flickering lights and frantic tone of the sirens swiftly cleared the road ahead. A few seconds later, the police car and fire rescue truck came to a stop behind the tangled vehicles.

Three paramedics piled out and quickly joined the policemen surveying the accident. A policeman stopped and began speaking to a group of bystanders. Then, turning, he pointed toward the plumbing-supply store, and the three paramedics rushed over to examine the injured man, who was still holding the paper towels to his forehead. Within a few more minutes, another patrol car drove by us, and a large fire truck pulled up and began unfurling the thick fabric-lined hoses that were neatly stacked on the top of the truck. I watched as they hurriedly hosed down the street around the fused cars. Spectators frantically moved farther away as the firemen aggressively sprayed the highway.

The policemen had split up, and one was talking to the young driver and the other to the man receiving assistance from the paramedics. The young man, who I assumed had been the driver of the second car, seemed to be nervous, and I could see he was quite upset. The injured man was sitting slumped over on a parking curb and seemed somber as the paramedics worked on his forehead. I watched the policemen as they took notes, occasionally typing on their tablets. Another officer had pulled up and had a tape measure out and was measuring here and there. I assumed he was measuring the skid marks and documenting the positions of the vehicles.

I saw that Raffie was also intently watching the scene down the street as it continued to unfold. I could see he was looking at the patrol officers as they performed their duties. Another police vehicle pulled up, and an officer in a yellow vest got out. He adjusted the vest as he walked ahead of the crumpled cars. He immediately took charge and began directing traffic around the collision with hand motions and his whistle.

"I imagine it's tough to be a police officer today," the old man said quietly, as if he was talking to himself. He then turned toward me and calmly said, "These officers have to deal with incidents like this every day, and then their next call might be a bank robbery in process or a domestic violence situation or a drive-by shooting. Hopefully they receive a lot of training. It's a tough job, and I don't think they get the credit they deserve."

"Yeah," I said. "It's a job I wouldn't want to do. I have a hard job at times, but I don't have to worry about being shot at or stabbed."

"It's a shame today that some people don't support them," the old man lamented, turning back toward the accident scene. "It reminds me of when I got back from the war in Vietnam. It's a terrible feeling when you are just doing your job and people don't respect you. And I know there are some bad cops, but I understand the vast majority are good and just want to serve and protect the public."

As I watched the first responders performing their duties, I said, "I know there are bad actors in every profession. Even in banking."

"But Paul, unfortunately the good ones get tarred and feathered with the actions of the bad ones. I have some hope that it will get better. We just need to swing back toward the center. Maybe someday there will be no bad cops. But we can't prevent law enforcement officers from doing their jobs. If we do, society will suffer. And the communities needing the most protection will be hurt the most."

The old man continued, "You know, there's always going to be crime to combat. There's always going to be bad guys. And really, it's a small percentage of people who commit crimes. I've heard that repeat offenders commit most of the crimes. I have a friend who is a judge in a small town in Colorado, and he told me that over sixty percent of the crime suspects brought before him each day are suspects he has seen multiple times before in his courtroom."

"I have heard that also," I said. "A lot of repeat offenders. But how do we reduce crime without taking away the rights of the repeat offenders? Do we make the punishments more severe? Do we incarcerate these repeat offenders with longer prison sentences?"

"Don't get me wrong," said the old man. "I'm not for locking anybody up and throwing away the key. And I believe in giving every man or woman a second chance in life. However, if they never stop getting in trouble and creating hardships for law-abiding citizens, they should spend more time in jail. Society can only be patient for so long. We need to use some common sense here. And unfortunately, we have to understand that there are some people who just can't be rehabilitated."

"I suppose you're right, Raffie. I guess sometimes you just can't change the spots on a leopard."

"We are fortunate," the old man continued, "to live in such a free society that everybody can make their own decisions and choices and mistakes. But one has to be a responsible citizen and work to better oneself and do the right things. There have to be consequences for repeatedly breaking the law."

The injured man was now standing up and was being escorted slowly by the paramedics to their emergency rescue vehicle. His head was heavily bandaged, and his shirt displayed the large amount of blood he had lost from his head wound.

"They are taking that man to the hospital," I observed. "I wonder if he also got a concussion."

The old man answered, "As hard as the cars hit, I wouldn't be surprised if he had a concussion."

The spectators were slowly dissolving into their vehicles in the late-afternoon heat. The policemen continued to work at the accident scene, and a tow truck had arrived to disengage the two vehicles.

I watched as a bright red sports car passed by us and pulled off the road behind the remaining police cars. A tall middle-aged man with graying hair got out and slowly walked toward the accident. He walked cautiously, avoiding the slow-moving traffic as he surveyed the scene. I could see he was inspecting the damage to the interlocked cars. He then proceeded over to the policeman who was still talking to the young driver. The other two young occupants were standing behind the driver, quietly listening as the officer conducted his inquiry.

I could see that the young driver knew the approaching man, as he looked up and immediately began talking to him. The officer also turned around to acknowledge the gentleman. As the group stood there, I thought this could be the driver's father. The age differential seemed about right.

The young driver gestured to the melded cars, and I could see he was beginning to get emotional again. The tall middle-aged man began talking to him, and after a while, the young man just quit talking and hung his head down. The young man looked to be very despondent. At that moment I saw the tall man, presumably the father, move closer and place his arm around his son, and he appeared to be comforting him.

Seeing the man comforting his son made me recall my first accident. It happened when I was in high school. I drove to school each day using the family car. On one morning, not being an experienced driver, I took a chance making a left turn into incoming traffic. A little sports car had darted behind a large delivery truck, and I did not see it. We collided, and I clearly recall the shock of wrecking the family car. It was a major traumatic moment I will never forget. I called my parents afterward, and I remember being incredibly apologetic and emotional. I remember telling my father I would work and pay for the damage. My father usually was not a tremendously understanding man, but for some reason he did not react adversely. All he asked was "Are you all right?" and "Did anyone get hurt?" Fortunately, there were no injuries to anyone, though the sports car driver at the scene was quite upset with the neophyte driver.

I watched as the tow truck driver worked to separate the vehicles. The firemen stood idle along the roadside, watching the tow truck driver applying chains to the axle of one of the damaged cars. The officer in the yellow vest was still directing traffic around the collision. Another man who had arrived with the tow truck driver was vigorously sweeping broken glass and plastic car pieces off the road.

Suddenly, I heard a deep booming sound from somewhere, echoing like a muffled bass drum. I could tell from the sound that it was not far away, and it caught me by surprise. I turned and quickly asked the old man in disbelief, "That sounded like thunder. Was that thunder?"

"Yes, it was. We will likely get some rain this afternoon and evening. This is our rainy season."

I stared amusedly at the dusty, parched parking lot in front of me. If this was the rainy season, what must the dry season look like? I couldn't imagine what the ground would look like if there was a real drought. Literally all day long, the arid, desiccated parking lot silt had shifted and swirled with any hint of a breeze. And occasionally it had caused a flurry of parched dust to rise high in the air over the highway.

"You really get much rain around here?" I asked, still not believing it could rain.

"Not a lot for most of the year. But the next two months we will get our rain."

The sudden sound of thunder seemed to accelerate the activity of the tow truck operator and his assistant. They had dislodged the two cars and were attaching a cable to one of the vehicles to hoist it up on the bed of the tow truck. I watched as they slowly winched up the vehicle. I could hear the winch laboring to pull the car up the incline of the truck bed. The other damaged car was sitting on the side of the road and was no longer blocking the traffic. The officer in the yellow vest was still motioning the traffic forward as the backup of vehicles slowly began to dissipate.

I heard another low booming sound that was clearly closer to us. It was a rolling, thunderous sound like a sustained beating on timpani drums. A few seconds later, the next pitch of rolling thunder caused the porch to shake under my feet. I could tell the storm was not far from us. The old man did not appear to be bothered by the increasing tempo of thunder and sat contentedly watching the men finishing their work on the highway.

The tow truck men were securing the winched vehicle to the truck bed. I watched as they hurriedly scampered around the bed of the truck making sure the car was properly anchored onto the deck of the tow truck. Occasionally they would tug at a chain or unfasten and tighten a strap. I could see that the other chains that had previously been used to detach the cars were still lying along the shoulder of the highway in the sparse grass.

The traffic resumed its normal pace in front of the grocery. I watched as the tow truck roared to life, snorting black smoke upward from its twin tailpipes on each side of the cab. Slowly the truck turned and accelerated away, leaving behind the remaining damaged car for a later pickup.

The officers had completed their assessment and recording of the accident and were climbing back into their vehicles. The three teenagers followed the driver's father quietly back to his car with their heads down. At this distance, the father looked like a mother duck leading a group of fledglings across the highway. Not once did they look up at the passing vehicles as they somberly slumped into the car. The father took one last look up the road and down before climbing into the driver's seat. The car then bounced up onto the pavement, accelerating, leaving a completely peaceful scene as if nothing tumultuous had ever happened.

Just up the highway, I could see a mounting wall of dark clouds.

SAGE OF LAS CRUCES

*****

I knew my car was really close to being ready to drive again. I could see that Diego had pulled the car outside and was sitting in the driver's seat. He was accelerating the engine and looking down at the dashboard panel. I assumed he was checking to make sure the dashboard readings were where they should be.

The old man turned toward me to speak. And at that moment a strong gust of wind ruffled his hair as he said, "Paul, you know, I love the feeling and sensation of an approaching thunderstorm."

"It is exhilarating," I answered as the wind began to pick up, blowing more consistently across the highway. I could feel the kinetic energy and mass of the approaching storm that filled the darkening sky above the porch. I could see out on the highway the dust being pushed up into the air. A paper cup was bouncing and skidding along the highway from the force of the wind.

The old man continued, "I have to say one of the greatest spectacles in nature is seeing a menacing derecho storm coming toward you out on the vast, flat West Texas prairie. It's quite incredible to see the immensity and energy in the atmosphere building and the dark wall of clouds approaching you. And on the prairie, you see it in full panorama, with nothing blocking your sight. No trees, no buildings, and no mountains. You can smell the rain in the air when the wind begins to pick up. And you can literally feel the drop in air pressure. I've seen this spectacle many times on the open prairie and a few times at sea. I never get tired of feeling that energy in the air. The energy of an approaching thunderstorm is so real and palpable, and no matter how old I get, it still feels invigorating."

I heard the intensity in Raffie's voice as he relished his euphoric feeling of watching an approaching storm on the open prairie. I could see him as a younger man standing on an oil derrick, waving his hard hat to the sky in defiance of the immensity of nature. It just seemed natural that he would enjoy that.

"Paul, another sense of nature I have always enjoyed is the smell of new-cut grass. When I was just barely a teenager, I would mow lawns for older people on our street to make some money. I had about twenty or so customers, and I made two dollars a mowing. And I paid for the gas and used my mower. It was a lot of work in the summer heat. But two dollars went a lot further then."

"And your gas was cheaper then also," I noted.

"Yeah, only thirty cents a gallon," he chuckled to himself. "But I remember that smell of new-cut grass. Especially if I mowed in the morning when the dew was still on the lawns. I have to say I haven't smelled new-cut grass in many years. You know, there isn't as much grass around here to cut."

I thought that here was another example of Raffie's work ethic. Even when he was barely a teenager, he was mowing lawns and earning an income. Early on he had developed his entrepreneurial spirit. It was no wonder, and it should not have been a surprise, that he had been so financially successful in his life.

"Paul, I do like a good meal, even though I am not a good cook."

Well, that's a random thought, I mused to myself.

"But Paul, the food today doesn't seem to taste as good as it did when I was younger. My grandmother was a great cook. She made the best *enmolada* I ever tasted. It was so good. I can still remember the texture and blending of the mole and cheese and shredded chicken. She could have opened up a restaurant and done quite well." Raffie's voice trailed off, and he suddenly looked somber while recalling the memories of his grandmother. "You know, she didn't have much, and I wish I could have done more to help her. The best I could do for her at that time was keeping her house up and fixing things for her." He looked up into the sky. "She passed away when I was seventeen."

As he spoke, I recalled the passing of my grandparents and how that had affected me. I said, "Raffie, my grandparents on my mother's side passed away when I was in high school. On my father's side, my grandparents passed away well before I was born. My grandma and grandpa were the first close people that passed away in my life that I can remember. Their memories have stuck with me, and I even see them in my dreams every now and then."

Raffie looked over at me and turned his body to look me in the eye. "You know, I believe they watch us," he said in a serious tone. "I've always felt in my life that I had a guardian angel watching over me. I never felt alone or without hope. I know I'm being protected from above."

I had not had that feeling in my life, but I understood how comfortable that must feel. I must confess that at times when something really significant was out of my control, I had found myself asking for help from a benevolent deity removed from my reality. It did give me a sense of hope that somehow things would get better and something would happen.

The old man continued conversing and reminiscing about his grandmother. He spoke now with an affectionate tone in his voice. "I would visit my grandmother after school all the time, and she knew I had a large appetite. She would always have something freshly prepared for me to eat."

"Raffie, I guess she wanted to please you." I was thinking she must have felt a maternal, caring instinct toward him as a grandson. "She must have been a real nice grandmother."

"Yes, she was," he said. "You know, just last week a good friend of mine brought me a dish of *enmolada*. Her husband had told her I loved it and that I hadn't had it in years. It was so thoughtful and kind of her." He stopped, and I could see from his hesitation that he was contemplating the words he was next going to say. "It was so nice of her to bring that meal to me. I thanked her profusely and told her how delicious it was. But Paul, it just didn't taste the same as how I remembered it should taste. I'm sure it had all the same ingredients and was well prepared. But it just didn't taste the same."

"Maybe your grandmother had a secret ingredient?"

"That's probably true." He smiled to himself. "Or maybe my taste buds have just changed over the years."

*****

We were now totally enveloped in the darkness of the storm. The large, dark clouds boiled upward in the sky as the storm ominously threatened the peacefulness of the day. I thought the way the rain arrived here in New Mexico was very dissimilar to what I experience in Seattle. We get days of rain and massive cloud cover. We do not see thunderstorms like this one that build during the day when the heat is so oppressive. I remember being in Florida once on a vacation and seeing every afternoon, at about the same time, the tall white clouds turning dark, developing into mountainous thunderstorms.

Suddenly a flash of white light brightened the sky to my left. As I turned, I heard the trailing clap of thunder. I judged that it was not more than a second between the flash and the sound of thunder.

The old man did not appear to be bothered by the flash of light or the subsequent thunder. Or he may have just ignored it. I could see that his eyes were focused directly ahead as the vehicles sped by on the highway, trying to outrace the storm. At the same time, the cars driving in the opposite direction were driving right into the teeth of the storm.

I was aware I had only a short time left to converse with Raffie. I still felt I needed to understand in a deeper way how this man had been able to transcend his very poor beginning to reach his present life. He had begun in life well below where most begin and ended well above where most end.

I turned toward him and directly asked, "Raffie, did you ever think that you wouldn't be where you are today?" This was a question I would not usually have asked of anyone unless I had known them for a while. But having listened to the old man throughout the day, I sensed he would be comfortable answering this question. And I added, "I mean, achieving what you have achieved?"

The old man pondered my question for a moment and then rocked forward in his chair. The bend in his back was now more pronounced than before. It seemed like the burden of many days of hard work and personal tragedies still weighed on his back as he contemplated my question.

"Let me say," he began slowly, "that I am content with my life even though I live alone now and wish Marcia was still here with me. There were many years of hard work, many prayers, and unending stress that built my life. And I have not many more years left. As to where I am, I feel my path was chosen for me. I feel that in my life I have received many bountiful blessings, and now I can share my blessings with others. As I said earlier, Paul, from those to whom much is given, much is expected. I do not see anything that I've obtained as belonging only to me. I am blessed, and it is my responsibility now to help others."

I was moved by the old man's sincerity and genuineness. He had a very likable humbleness in his words and spoke without any hubris. I think he sincerely and firmly believed what he had just said. His solid faith and providential belief were the static core of his life, without any garnishment or embellishment. His take on life was humbling to me as well. He spoke as if he was only a caretaker of the many blessings he had received. But at the same time, as a steward of those abundant blessings he had received, he knew it was required and paramount for him to share those blessings with others. It was an admirable quality, and I had never met anyone before who could address that sentiment without being entangled in self-interest or self-promotion.

From the corner of the porch overhang, I saw another flash of lightning, which was followed by a crack of thunder. The rain would be coming soon, and I could smell it in the air. The wind blew stronger across the porch and the parking lot. Great clouds of dust now blew across the parking lot, masking the highway. For the first time all day, with the sudden drop in temperature and pickup of the wind, it felt very comfortable sitting on the porch. It was a pleasurable respite from the heat.

"You know, not all people who have done as well as you think like you do," I said in earnestness. "I mean, you are very genuine and exemplify how Americans should live their lives in this free country. You aren't boastful or like some people today who are so full of themselves. You don't blame others for your mistakes or take credit for the favorable things in your life that you assert are providential. That's really unusual in today's world."

The old man sat with his hands in his lap and slowly lifted his head to speak. "I cannot change anyone or criticize anyone who may have a big ego or be boastful about the blessings they've received. I can only speak for myself and change my attitude. I believe one does not need to have a spotlight on oneself when one does something truly virtuous. Giving back to people in need should be expected. It should not be viewed as a personal triumph. I believe the term today applied to some is *virtue signaling*. They do things wanting recognition that they are good and nice people. But there are a lot of truly good people out there who you never hear about. People that give back to their communities and support good causes without wanting to be recognized. And some of these people don't have much of anything to give but their time."

The old man attempted to shift his body in the chair as he had done before. It seemed like he was trying to get more comfortable as he spoke. I studied his face now against the dark backdrop of the sky. The wrinkles and deep furrows and lines were not as observable. The years of toil and hardship carved into his face were cloaked under the dark sky. And as he spoke, he continued in a reflective, pleasant tone.

"Paul, as you know, I grew up poor, really poor. And the community we lived in was poor as well. I can tell you that there were many people in that community who didn't have a lot and still gave to help their neighbors who truly needed help. And many of them had difficult jobs, and sometimes two jobs, and they still managed to volunteer to help others. They didn't tell the world what they were doing. They may have had little, but they helped others that were truly in need. Paul, these people are the truly virtuous people in this world."

I nodded, affirming what he had said. "Yes, I imagine there are a lot of unrecognized good people in this world. As you say, truly virtuous people who give a lot more of themselves than those who have received a lot from this world."

"The salt of the earth. Paul, do you know what that means?"

I responded, "People that are just common people who are genuine and work to provide for their families and communities."

The old man leaned toward me and corrected me in a fatherly tone. "Paul, I wouldn't say they are common people. There is nothing common about these people."

"I didn't mean to insinuate they were unimportant when I said common," I recanted. "As you said, they are truly virtuous people."

The old man leaned back in his chair again. "Paul, as I said, the people who give freely to others and work hard for their families and communities are the salt of the earth. They are net givers rather than net receivers. They are understanding and kind people who want to help others without personally standing out in the crowd. If a neighbor needs help, they are there. If their community needs help, they are there. If our country needs them to serve, they are there.

You know, Paul, salt was a very valuable commodity in most cultures for thousands of years. The Egyptians used it for religious purposes, as a gift to the gods. Salt was used for healing wounds, preserving food, and flavoring food, and it was even used as money for trade." The old man stopped to clear his throat. "Paul, salt was extremely cherished. So the expressions 'salt of the earth' and that someone is 'worth their weight in salt' have a deeper meaning. They place a high value on someone christened with these terms."

I nodded, as I fully understood what he meant. "Raffie, I think most people don't realize what those expressions mean. Most people today think that 'salt of the earth' defines countrified people, gullible people, and hayseeds."

"Yes, they are a misunderstood bunch," the old man said. "This is why these folks are not common people. They are exceptional, caring people. I truly believe I am fortunate if someone considers me to be one of them."

I had met a few people in my life that had the characteristics that Raffie defined as being the salt of the earth. One couple I met once up in the mountains where my dad had his lake house were truly genuine, caring people. I remember that once when a large pine tree fell on my dad's storage shed in the backyard, this couple came over to help him. They brought their chain saws and cut the tree into pieces and afterward helped my dad repair the shed. They enjoyed helping him out and felt it was their neighborly duty to do so. The helping couple was well intentioned, and they didn't expect anything in return for their help. I heard later they had done similar unselfish deeds for several other neighbors.

"Paul, those among us that are selfish with their time and resources or are boastful or not willing to care for their families and communities, they are not worth their weight in salt and are not the salt of the earth."

As the old man continued, I could tell from the twinkle in his eyes that he strongly believed in these qualities he cherished in people—and that he personally felt responsible and obligated to live up to the standards of the people who possessed these qualities.

"You asked me before, Paul, 'Did you ever think you wouldn't be where you are today?' That is an easy question for me to answer. Yes, I never thought I'd be where I am today. I am blessed that I was given some skills and a drive to work. And I always viewed my life as a fragile crucible that was a gift. Anything of value that I put into my life, I was obligated to earn a return on, whether that was by completing my schooling, starting a company, or just working hard. I could not in all conscience hide and bury my gifts and blessings. Working hard for me also included trying to be a loving husband and father and caring about my neighbors and friends. I don't think I did everything as well as I should've, but I tried.

"Paul, unfortunately today we are surrounded by certain individuals, that have reached the pinnacle of their profession, and who attribute their success solely to themselves. They possess no traits that would in the least be considered noble or belonging to the salt of the earth. They accumulate wealth and at the same time admonish the wealthy. Maybe from a sense of guilt or just a lack of self-awareness. They only value money, their self-image, and their status in society. As I said before the worst of these are the elitists among us. They may be celebrities, sports figures, or politicians. All may be considered as actors oblivious to their hypocrisy. They constantly pander to their reputations and try to look virtuous, as long as they get recognized by society for their deeds. They are modern-day Pharisees. Maybe they even volunteer a few days a year and throw a little bit of their money at a cause. But it's all about themselves, their reputation and self-image. They make hollow statements with no substantial support backing their beliefs. They parrot one another and try to appear more virtuous than one another. They are charlatans selling their words of piety to society. But it is only acting, with very little action to back up their good words. Paul, do you know what the Greek word for 'actor' is?"

"I don't know," I answered.

"Paul, the Greek word for 'actor' is *hypocrite*. These people wear masks, pretending to be something else. They are pretending to be something they are not. Are they not hypocrites?"

"I suppose," I answered, as the sound of thunder echoed down the street. "But I don't know them personally."

"Yes, I don't either. But people are usually remembered for who they truly are," said the old man. "Over time very few entertainers and sports figures are remembered, and the vast majority are forgotten. In two to three generations, most of the names in music, movies and television, and even sports are not remembered and are virtually forgotten. Each generation creates its own popular icons. But truly good people will be remembered in history. History christens the truly virtuous people favorably. On the other hand, the pontificating elitists whose personal lives are in conflict with their spoken beliefs will likely be forgotten. Some may even be remembered for their many contradictions, hypocrisies, and mistakes."

"There are plenty of examples of that," I said. "Documentaries love to focus on the negative aspects of a politician's or a celebrity's character and the mistakes they've made in their lives."

"You know the old expression 'Actions always speak louder than words'?" Raffie said, looking at me. "It gets down to how you want to be remembered. What do you want your genuine legacy to be? Or not to be? And I mean genuine legacy, not pretending to be someone you are not.

I fear today we are losing what it means to be an American. We are replacing the values associated with the salt of the earth with a new order of elitism that cherishes greed, accumulating wealth, self-indulgence, vanity, and arrogance. But these personal character flaws in this new rise in elitism are cloaked and hidden behind virtuous words and hollow actions."

*****

The time between the flashes of lightning and the rolling thunder was diminishing as the rain began to fall. I could feel a firm and sustained breeze again blowing across the porch. I watched a swirl of parched sand pick up from the parking lot, twist in a circle, and then dissipate. I thought, *Is this what they call a dust devil down here?*

"Raffie, it's starting to rain," I said as I watched the dotting of sprinkles hitting the dry parking lot. "Should we move inside?"

"No, Paul, we should be OK. The rain will not reach us." He looked down at the floor of the porch and pointed to a spot. "It will go as far as that third plank and no farther."

Larger and more frequent raindrops were now striking the dry parking lot. "This rain is so good for us," Raffie said. "It was so dry this past winter and spring. I just hope we don't have any flooding in town."

The sky grew even darker, and the rain began to intensify. The headlights from each vehicle that passed in front of the small grocery now illuminated the highway. As each vehicle passed by us, I could see the futile efforts of the windshield wipers attempting to push the driving rain off the windshields. As the volume and force of the rain continued to increase, the parking lot was being peppered with thousands of impacts. Each raindrop spattered in all directions, leaving a deep crater in the dry dust. The rain was now striking the porch railing in front of me. True to Raffie's words, it looked like no rain was going to reach us where we sat on the porch. It appeared the rain would not proceed beyond the third plank.

At that moment a customer who had been inside came running out in full stride, slamming the screen door behind him. He scooted down the steps, carrying a bag of groceries in each arm. He slipped slightly on the final step but caught himself. Splashing his way to his car, he slid the grocery bags onto the front seat, and in a fluid athletic feat he jumped inside, closing the door behind him in one motion. I could see his hair was matted down with the rain, and he was wiping his face with his hand to clear his vision. As the man started the car, the wipers threw an enormous wave of water off each side of the windshield.

"He is lucky," I said, looking at the man in the car. "I thought for a moment he was going to slip and fall."

"Yes, I thought for a moment he was going to fall also," the old man said. "I was ready to get up and help him if he fell."

I thought to myself that it was probably not a good idea for Raffie to be trying to pick up the man while standing in a rainstorm. I could see both of them lying in the mud, with groceries scattered everywhere. The old man would be trying to pick up one grocery item at a time while the grocery bags disintegrated in the rain. Maybe thirty years ago he could have done it, but not today, I mused.

The force of the rain now grew to a constant intensity. I shuddered as a clap of thunder shook the deck. The parking lot was a miasma of arid sand and water. As the rain fell, small rivers of water flowed toward the deck, pooling in larger and larger puddles. Large raindrops were spattering on the top of the porch railing in front of me, shooting rays of moisture in each direction. Above me the rainwater flowed off the roof like a waterfall, cascading down to the muddy parking lot.

"This will be a short rain," Raffie said, looking up at the dark sky. "When the rain falls like this, it doesn't last long."

"This is like a monsoon," I said, raising my voice to be heard above the sound of the rain.

Raffie chuckled. "Not truly like the rains we got in Southeast Asia. But we do get some violent thunderstorms here."

It continued pouring for about ten minutes, and then the sun broke though the cloud cover, and the storm quickly disappeared. As quickly as the rain had come, it went away. This again reminded me of being in Florida. The rain would build to an intensity and then just as quickly dissipate. The air would cool a bit in Florida afterward, but I wasn't so sure if that would happen here with the lower humidity.

The pools of standing water in the parking lot were quickly disappearing, and what was left was a drying mud base. On the road I could see steam rising from the asphalt as the rainwater evaporated into the atmosphere.

Miggy opened the screen door and poked his head out. As he surveyed the parking lot he said, "Well, that should cool off everything for a short while. Gentlemen, I'm working on your sandwiches and will bring them out when they are ready."

*****

A big pickup truck pulled up in the parking lot, and a man got out and began trudging through the quickly solidifying mud. He was a tall, thin black man, middle-aged, wearing work clothes and a military fatigue hat. His shoulders were broad, and his arms were muscled. I figured he either worked out a lot at a gym or had done a lot of heavy lifting in his life. He walked toward the steps with his head down. His leather boots were covered in mud, which extended up to and onto the bottom hem of his work jeans.

He carefully stepped out of the mud onto the bottom step of the deck. I watched him as he looked up and smiled at Raffie.

"Hey, Raffie, how are you today?" he asked, greeting the old man. I was struck by the contrast between this man's physical stature and the softness in his voice.

Raffie looked up and returned a smile. "I'm fine, Ray. How is your dad doing today?"

The man looked down at the deck, and a change almost instantly came over him. I watched as his expression transformed suddenly from a pleasant, rested look to an exhausted appearance. His arms hung loosely by his side now, and his neck began to droop as he looked down at his feet. "Dad is not doing well, Raffie. We had to call hospice in yesterday." I could see the sadness in this man's downcast eyes. He stopped and took his hat off in what appeared to be a respectful gesture toward the old man. "It's not good."

"I'm sorry to hear that, Ray," the old man answered with a sympathetic tone of sadness in his voice. "Your dad's a good man. I have a deep respect for him and everything he's done. As you know, he's been a friend and a part of my life for many years."

"Raffie, he says the same thing about you. You know you are like kin to us."

I could see Raffie's face as he looked at the man, and suddenly moisture appeared in the corners of his dark eyes. "That means a lot," he said in a soft, low voice, and he asked, "Ray, is there anything I can do to help you all?"

Ray looked up at Raffie and answered, "Just pray for us. We don't need anything but prayer for the family and Dad."

"I can do that," Raffie said. "Is it possible if I could come by early tonight and visit him?"

I could see it was difficult for the man to answer. He simply nodded quietly, indicating it was all right to do so. "I think he would like that," he finally said. "He would like a visit from you." Ray turned now toward the screen door and said, "Raffie, I just came here to pick up some soup for him. It's the only thing he'll eat, if he eats anything."

Even though I didn't know this man's father, I felt I had to say something to his distraught son at this moment. "I'm sorry to hear your father is not doing well," I began sympathetically. "It sounds like he is a good man."

Raffie now turned slowly toward me and pointed, saying, "Ray Junior, this is Paul. He's waiting on Diego to fix his car. He's been a pleasant companion all day."

As Ray turned to look at me, I could see the deep anguish across his face. He spoke slowly in a solemn and sincere tone. "Nice to meet you, Paul." He then slowly turned back to Raffie and said, "You know Dad has worked so hard his whole life. I hope I can be half the man he is."

The old man picked up his head now as high as he could and looked directly into Ray's eyes as he spoke. "Ray, you're a good son. Your dad, I know, is proud of all of you. I don't think the apple has fallen far from the tree."

"Thank you, Raffie, for saying those kind words," Ray responded, his voice quivering. I thought to myself that the son was trying to keep it together emotionally. And I fully understood the feeling.

"Son, please tell your dad I will come by tonight and that I'm praying for him and your family."

"I will."

Raffie asked, "How is the ranch doing?"

"We now have over three thousand head of cattle in the field and still more birthing. Dad just bought another hundred and ten acres."

"Your dad is a smart rancher," said Raffie. "I think you all have the best ranch anywhere around here."

"Thank you," Ray answered. "I don't know if there is a man who has ever worked as hard as my dad to make it so. At eighty-seven he was still mending fences last summer in the hot afternoon sun and replacing posts using his old metal tamper. We all tried to convince him to use the gas-powered tamper the rest of us used. But he wouldn't budge."

The son began to smile as he recalled his father's obstinate, old-school style of working the fence line. I gathered that his father was not only a hard worker but also determined to do things the way he wanted to do things.

"Ray, I think your dad's work has allowed him to live this long." Raffie paused to cough inside his elbow. "Your whole family has done well. Does your sister still own that fancy dress shop in Amarillo?"

"Yeah, she is a real go-getter," Ray answered. "She just finished providing all the dresses for four big weddings. She's here now. The whole family is here now."

Ray moved slowly toward the screen door. "Raffie, I guess I better get inside and get dad's soup." He looked at the both of us now and said, "He can get cranky if he decides he wants to eat something. He especially likes chicken soup."

I watched as Ray went inside the grocery. I noticed that he seemed careful to close the door quietly behind him.

Not much later the screen door opened, and Ray emerged with a small brown bag. He stopped and turned toward us to say something. But at that moment, before he could speak, I heard an unfamiliar cell phone ring. Ray reached into the front pocket of his jeans and pulled out a cell phone. Holding it to his ear, he said, "Hey."

As he held the phone, I could see his eyes slowly close, and a tear began to run down the right side of his face. He continued to listen and then spoke with his voice breaking up. "Yes, he did live a long life. But honey, it is still so sad. I will be home shortly." His voice trailed off as he ended the call. I suddenly felt a deep sympathetic kinship toward Ray. A kinship of the sorrow everyone eventually will have in their lives when someone close to them passes away. Ray quietly pushed the phone back into his pocket. He was looking down, and I could see his mouth now begin to contort into a painful grimace as tears began rushing uncontrollably down his cheeks.

Raffie got up slowly, bracing himself on the arms of his chair. He slowly moved toward the grieving son and embraced him, with his arms around the man's back. Ray Junior seemed to wilt into his arms, and the old man said in a comforting tone, "It's OK, son. It's tough. I know. I've lost my parents and a wife, and I know. Your dad's in heaven now. He's a child of God."

"I know, Raffie," the man responded through his tears. "But I'll miss him so much. He's my dad."

"I know you will miss him. But he will be with you in spirit. I think about my wife every day. I miss her so much. Just know that your dad was special, and he'd want you to continue doing good things. You're his legacy."

The old man moved back toward his chair. The son began rubbing his eyes. "Thank you, Raffie," he said, clearing his throat. "It's just such a shock, even when you knew it was coming."

The old man nodded silently and then looked squarely into the eyes of Ray Junior and said, "Please let me know where and when the service will be held. I want to be there with you and the family. And son, again, if there is anything else I can help you or your family with, please let me know."

Ray answered, still wiping the tears from his face, "I will, Raffie. I will."

I watched Ray Junior as he turned and walked down the steps. His shoulders were heavier now, and his head had sunk down between his broad shoulders. He carried the small brown bag containing the can of soup in his right hand. I found myself again feeling very sad for Ray and his family as he trudged back to his truck in the mud.

Ray Junior climbed into the pickup and reached down to start the engine. As the truck roared to life, he looked up and gave us an affectionate, thankful wave. Tears were still running down his face. As Ray backed the truck up slowly, I could see the treads on the tires were covered in mud. The truck moved forward, climbing up onto the highway. As it ran down the road, the wheels sprayed a shower of mud onto the asphalt. Soon the truck was out of sight.

We sat there silent for a moment. I could see the old man rubbing the sides of his face on the cuff of his shirt.

He had been quite voluble most of the day but was now quiet, mourning his friend. Finally, looking at the sky, he said, "Life is so short. So short."

I nodded but did not speak.

"There are good people in this world," the old man began slowly, still staring up at the sky. "And there are really good people. Ray Senior I put in the last group. He was truly the salt of the earth."

For several more minutes, the old man sat in silence. Then he began to talk again. His voice took on an affectionate tone as he spoke about his friend. "Paul, I've been a friend of Ray Senior for many years. Since about forty years ago, I guess. Wait—it was more like forty-three. No, maybe forty-four years ago, as I recollect. I was still working for the big oil company then. I was driving up one evening to see several rigs I was managing in Chaves County. I was passing through this area, coming from some rigs I was in charge of south of here. I remember it was a very cold evening, and I hit a patch of ice, and my truck skidded off the road. It happened so fast I couldn't stop the skid. The truck ended up sideways in a ditch off the shoulder of the road. It took me a while to wiggle out of the door of the truck."

The old man stopped to clear his throat. "I was in the middle of nowhere. Nothing but ranchland and cattle as far as you could see. This was well before the days of cell phones. I couldn't call for help. And it was getting colder and darker. I just stood there on the road not knowing what to do next. My left arm was broken, but I didn't know that until I was taken to the hospital later. And I had a few cuts on me as well. There was a ranch road about fifty yards up the road from where I was standing. I remember I was beginning to shake a little bit, probably more from the shock of what had happened than the cold. Then, like a miracle, a pickup truck appeared, coming out of the ranch entrance that was just up the road.

"Paul, it was a blessing. The driver saw me and turned in my direction, and he pulled off across the road where I was standing. A man got out of the truck and approached me. That man was Ray Senior. He came over and surveyed the situation and told me to get in his truck. He drove me all the way into town and to a hospital. He arranged a wrecker to get my truck out of the ditch that night while I was still getting fixed up.

"He waited at the hospital until the cast was put on, and then he took me back to his ranch, where I met his wife and his children. They put me up that night and fed me the next morning. I can remember Ray telling me, 'We're going to town now to get your truck back.' Sure enough, the truck was waiting for me—with a few dents, but drivable. I paid for everything, and I asked him if I could pay him for his trouble. He balked at that and said, 'I'm not going to take any money from you, brother. I hope you'd do the same thing for me and my family if you saw one of us on the side of the road in a ditch.'

"Paul, I never forgot Ray. Every year we'd exchange Christmas cards, and I'd call him and find out how he was doing. If I was driving through here, I would always stop at the ranch. They'd always feed me a spread of food. Erma, his wife, was a good cook. She passed away several years ago. Once we moved here, I was able to entertain his family. Now the kids are all grown up and have children of their own. I think it was a guardian angel that night that sent him to me."

I could see the deep sadness in the old man's eyes as he spoke. "I'll miss Ray. Paul, in your life you are lucky to have one good friend. I mean a really good friend. Someone who you can count on and who will be there by your side. Most people don't even have one good friend they can count on in tough times. Ray was a true good friend. A God-fearing man." The old man paused and looked toward me. "Paul, I can't get out as much as I used to with my mobility, but I did see him a week ago. I heard he wasn't doing well. I had to see him, and we talked about our friendship. So sad that he's gone. Ray never asked for nothing and never took nothing. He did it his way. He and his family built that ranch with their own hard work and smarts. Ray could be gruff and obstinate, but he was a kind man."

We sat there quietly together again, and I didn't feel I needed to break the silence. I felt that the old man needed to mourn the loss of his old friend. I did not want to interrupt his personal thoughts as he forlornly stared at the passing cars. Tears were still in his eyes.

*****

I could hear the old man's cell phone ringing again. This time he was slow to pull the phone out from his pocket. He looked down at the caller ID and quietly said, "I don't want to take this call now." He let it ring several more times until it stopped.

After a few more seconds, the phone started ringing again. "Darn it, I really don't want to talk business right now. But she's persistent."

Reluctantly the old man put the phone to his ear. "Hello, Meghan," he said softly.

He listened intently as he wiped the remaining tears from his eyes on his shirtsleeve. I could see clearly the glistening streaks of moisture that had trailed down through the crevices in his cheeks.

"Meghan, that's great," he said in a quiet, somber tone. "You've done really well. That price is more than I expected."

He listened and then added without any emotion in his voice, "No, I am happy. I am. You did good. I just got some bad news about a good friend of mine." He paused, listening to Meghan, and then said, "OK, Meghan, you take care too. Thank you. No, I don't need anything. I'll be all right. I'll call you tomorrow."

The old man dropped the phone to his lap and continued to stare at the cars going by. He had a blank, melancholy stare in his eyes. I watched as he slowly shut his eyes periodically in meditation. I started to feel sorry for Raffie in his time of grief. Here was a man I had not known yesterday, yet today I'd been drawn into his world, and I felt like he was someone I had known for years.

After a while I felt compelled to say something. I felt a need to comfort him and said, "Raffie, I've been thinking about what you said about having one truly good friend. Other than my wife, I can only think of one person I would say is truly a good friend."

My words seemed to penetrate through the old man's melancholy state, and he slowly turned to me and began, "Paul, you're lucky." Then he seemed to open up gradually through his doleful sorrow and continued speaking softly. "I knew a man many years ago down in Texas who had a restaurant and bar." He stopped for a moment and took out his handkerchief and wiped his face. "When I was in town and his restaurant was open, I would eat there almost every day for lunch. The food was great, and the prices were reasonable. The owner was a likable guy and had steady patrons. Everybody liked him, and he would socialize with his customers and give them free food and drinks on occasion to keep everyone happy. I heard he gave away so much food and drink he could barely stay in business. At Thanksgiving, I heard he would open the restaurant just for his customers who had no family nearby and who were going to spend the day alone by themselves. He would put out a massive Thanksgiving feast for them. And he opened the bar, giving everyone free drinks."

The old man's voice began to pick up some tempo as he described the kindness of this man. "I remember there was also a man in town that had had a stroke and needed help, and this guy and his wife put him up in their house and fed him until he recovered. Again, he and his wife were very caring people."

I watched as the old man shifted in his chair and cleared his throat. "But the restaurant one night caught fire and burned down. Everything he had invested in it was lost. I understand that with the insurance proceeds he was barely able to pay off the bank. A real bad situation. Paul, what happened next says a lot about his friends, or fair-weather friends. He and his wife had no income, since they relied on the restaurant for making a living. But very few people, if any, reached out to help them. Once there were no more free drinks and free food, his so-called friends moved on. I often wondered whatever happened to his wife and him.

I'm sure by now both have long since passed away. All they needed were some truly good friends to come and help them out."

*****

The sun was much lower in the sky now, and long shadows were blanketing the parking lot and edging onto the street. It was a bit more comfortable on the porch. I was pleasantly content to just sit there and watch the cars go by and listen to the old man as he shared the stories of his life and commonsense wisdom.

"Paul, have you ever heard the expression 'Only the good die young'?"

"Yes, I have," I answered. "Do you believe that?"

"No, I don't. There are many good people who live long lives. I know of many. And I know of many who were not so good and died young. They would never experience maybe getting married, maybe having children, maybe owning a house, or putting in the years on a job. I think of those people the most. The ones I knew in my youth that died young.

"Paul, I feel I'm truly blessed to still be living. There comes a time when one does not dread a birthday but feels blessed to have lived another year." He suddenly turned to me to make his point and said, "Never dread growing old.

Sure, it's difficult, but keep doing something. Share your time and wealth, volunteer, help your kids, do something good."

Raffie smiled at me now and said, "And Paul, as you grow old, you may be slower, have more aches and pains and a slower memory, but in your mind, you are still that twenty-five-year-old buck. Your thoughts and feelings of self don't change. You just have to learn your limitations." He chuckled. "If you don't know your limitations, that can be dangerous."

I smiled. "I'll remember what you just said when I hopefully get there."

"They say," Raffie began, "that you reach your prime in your mid-twenties—did you know that?"

I shook my head. "So I'm past my prime, I guess."

The old man chuckled again. "So it's all downhill after twenty-five. No, not really. As you know, life is very enjoyable after your mid-twenties. As maturity comes, you experience life in a different way."

The old man reflected on this last point. "Paul, life is a cycle. When you are young, you only think of yourself, as everything is provided to you. Then when you become a teenager, you are less self-assured and more aware of your self-image. You're driven by how you are perceived by your peers. Then you get into your twenties, and maybe on your own, and you experience a level of freedom you've not experienced before. You are able to do what you want, when you want, and not be responsible to anyone. And then you may find someone who you think is right, and you decide to settle down and get married. As you know, that's when things change in a big way. You and your spouse have to be dependent on each other. There is more responsibility and sharing of thoughts, desires in life, and goals. And then you may have a child, which changes things even more. Now you must be devoted to helping raise a child. You worry more and get less sleep. There is a tremendous responsibility in raising a child; it's a full-time job. You cannot do things that only you want to do. You have to be less selfish. You have to be there for the child and family. Then middle age gradually creeps in without you even being perceptive of it. And your child is a teenager. Then suddenly you realize that your parents have grown older and need your attention. Your responsibility for raising an adult, caring for aging parents, and keeping up with a demanding job becomes even more taxing. Then you enter old age, and you begin to slow down. You've retired and can do what you want, when you want to do it. You can either return to being selfish or help others with your free time. And then there is always the joy of grandchildren, if you have any."

I laughed out loud and said, "So that's life in a nutshell."

"Paul, eventually I hope and pray you will get where I am today. I can tell you that being retired is different from any other time in your life. You have responsibilities but are no longer on the treadmill and competing in the rat race. Your thoughts are not clouded with tasks and things that you have to do. The old man paused and slowly continued speaking philosophically. "But inevitably, Paul, you do move to a point, if you live long enough, where you are dependent on a spouse or a guardian for help. You resist it, but it is inevitable. Life goes full circle, and you become like a child again."

The old man paused and once again turned and looked me in the eye. "But the game of life can be fun. It is not the same for everyone. But if you work at it and make the right decisions in your life, you'll be happier and can enjoy life to the fullest. There is nothing to fear or dread about growing old. Consider it a blessing to reach old age. There are many surprises and challenges in life, and there are some sorrows, but there can be so many joys. You must always look forward with enthusiasm to the next day."

*****

The screen door opened, and Miggy came out holding in one hand two sandwiches wrapped in white paper. In the other hand he held two soft drink bottles. Miggy announced, "Gentlemen, here's your sandwiches. Raffie, I just got this bread in this afternoon, so it's really fresh. I think you'll like it." Miggy turned to me and said, "Raffie likes a little caffeine this time every day. It keeps him awake. So enjoy the soft drinks."

I watched as Raffie placed the soda bottle on the floor beside his chair. He slowly unwrapped the paper around the sandwich bag. Gradually the sandwich appeared, and he carefully removed it from the paper.

Miggy had now gone back inside, and the two of us sat consuming what would be our dinner meal. The sun was dropping in the sky behind us, and the lengthening shadows continued to creep over the highway in front of us. The traffic was busier as more trucks and cars passed, going south toward the city.

We finished our sandwiches, and I turned to the old man and said, "Raffie, thank you again for the sandwich and drink. I do appreciate it."

The old man smiled and said, "You're welcome. I have to say that you've been a pleasant companion today."

A pickup truck pulled up in front of us, and a young man and woman inside got out. They were dressed in jeans, and the man was wearing a cowboy hat. They appeared to be in their midtwenties. They were both olive complected and had dark, black hair. The man was wearing an untucked white T-shirt, and the woman was wearing a short-sleeved, light-colored blouse. I watched as the woman leaned back into the truck, reaching for something. She seemed to be talking to herself, and then I saw that she was slowly picking up an infant. She held the baby carefully against her shoulder.

I watched as they approached us, looking up at Raffie and smiling. Raffie appeared to recognize them and immediately greeted them. "Why hi, Mauricio and Maria. I see you brought us a visitor today?"

"Yes, we did," the young man said. "Little Ana."

They walked up the steps and onto the deck and stood in front of Raffie. The young woman held the baby tightly to her, and I could see the little baby's head sticking out from the tight swaddling. The infant had only a patch of dark hair on the very top of her head. She could not have been more than a few weeks old. The old man leaned forward to observe the child, and his voice grew very soft and childlike. "Ah, look at little Ana. She's so beautiful. And sleeping like a princess."

"For now, at least," the young man quipped.

"But not at three this morning," the young woman added, laughing. "She was wide awake at three this morning."

Raffie chuckled to himself in a grandfatherly tone. "I remember those days. So long ago for me."

The young man looked down at the deck floor, seeming to be a bit uncertain how to begin. He then looked up at his wife and turned to the old man and said, "Mr. Raffie, we have a special favor to ask." He hesitated and looked at his wife again. "Ana does not have a godfather. We were thinking, if you were OK with it, that you might be Ana's godfather."

The young mother quickly added, "If you do not want to do this, that is OK. It would be an honor to have someone like you be her godfather, Mr. Raffie. You are so kind and well-liked by everyone."

I watched as Raffie studied their faces. They were waiting with great expectation for his response. He began responding slowly in a measured tone to the both of them: "I do not have a problem being Ana's godfather. I would be honored. But are you two all right with me being such an old man and being her godfather? I mean, I will pass from here before she is a teenager. Is that acceptable?"

They both nodded together, understanding his concern, and the young father said, "We have given some thought about that, and we have no problem with that. She will know when she's older that a very respected member of our community was her godfather. That will mean more to her, and to us, and give her some confidence that she is special."

The young mother added, "You do so much for the cathedral and the community, and we can think of no other person we would trust outside of our family members to be Ana's godfather. Mr. Raffie, as I said, we would be honored if you would be Ana's godfather. You are a member of our church, and we want to bring Ana up in the church to be a good person and have morals and respect others."

The old man smiled and resolutely said, "Well then, I will be Ana's godfather. You can tell everyone that I have accepted this honor and will be a part of her life. I, too, see this as a responsibility to help your daughter in her life. I want her to be special, not because of me, but because she is yours and a child of God."

The young mother instinctively leaned down and hugged Raffie with her free arm. I could see some tears welling up in her eyes. "Thank you so much, Mr. Raffie. You have made us very happy."

The young father smiled and nodded appreciatively. "Mr. Raffie, yes, thank you so much. You have made both of us very happy."

Raffie spoke up loudly now with excitement in his voice and said, "I look forward to being at her christening. And as long as I'm living, other important times in her life."

The young couple smiled ear to ear and answered in unison, "You will be invited to every important event in her life. Thank you so much again."

After the young couple had left, Raffie turned to me and said, "I hope I can live up to their expectations. I will work hard to keep my commitment, but who knows how long God will keep me here."

*****

An old, dusty red pickup truck pulled up in the parking lot. The truck screeched to a sliding halt, and a profuse amount of dust rose in front of us and drifted ominously onto the porch. Raffie looked up, and I could see in his eyes a look of forbearance. He obviously recognized the driver, but he did not make any gestures toward the man who climbed out of the truck.

The man was in his mid-forties and appeared unkempt. His badly faded jeans and T-shirt were ragged looking, and he had cut off the sleeves of the T-shirt. His hair was dark black and tossed about like one would toss a salad. He had a thin mustache with some stubble on his chin.

Raffie gave a deep sigh. A sigh that one makes when dreading a task to be performed. The old man did not immediately speak or greet the approaching man.

I watched as the man looked up at Raffie and said cheerfully, "Hi, Uncle Raffie. How are you doing today?"

Raffie answered without any expression in his face or voice. "Doing fine. I see you still haven't fixed the headlight I gave you money to fix on your truck there. You know you can get fined for that."

The man seemed to ignore the warning. "I know. I know. Just haven't had the time to do that."

Raffie responded, "I bet you haven't. Did you take the job with Mr. Parsons that I set up for you?"

"I did," the man answered. "I worked there a while, but he's a hard person to work for."

"In what way?" Raffie asked.

"Well, to begin with he was always telling me how to stock his shelves. I mean, like really specific little things that were ridiculous. He was so unreasonable. Like everything had to be perfect with him. I just couldn't ever please the man."

I could see Raffie was getting agitated by his nephew's remarks. "You quit the job, José?"

"Well, not exactly," the nephew answered. "We came to a mutual agreement that I wasn't going to work out there. It was probably best for the both of us."

Raffie did not look at his nephew but was looking over him at the street. I could see he was trying to stay calm. "So what are you doing now?"

The nephew looked down at the deck and then looked up, slowly smiling at Raffie. "Well, I have a great opportunity down in Amarillo. A really good opportunity, you know. I can make some big money down there."

Raffie asked, "And what is the opportunity?"

The nephew looked away now into the distance, avoiding eye contact with the old man. He hesitated and then said, "Well, uh, it's an opportunity I think I would like and can do very well at. Like it involves selling things."

"Sales, huh. What are you selling?"

The nephew answered, "Imported goods. From all over the world."

"Really?" Raffie cleared his throat. "You've had quite a few jobs over the last twenty years that I can remember. And I don't recall you knowing anything about imported goods." Raffie stopped and abruptly admonished him: "And José, I am going to warn you now, if this job puts you back in jail, I'm not going to bail you out this time."

"Oh no, Uncle Raffie. This is all legit. I'm not getting into any trouble with this job."

Raffie sighed again. "If your dad was still living, he would be really worried about you. Just as I have been. José, I don't know if I can trust you anymore."

The nephew protested immediately, raising his voice. "You got to help me. I'm your blood, and I keep trying but don't get any luck. People are against me. I do my best, but people see me as a convict or nonwhite, and I get treated badly."

"Your dad did OK. Was he treated badly?"

"Well, he was lucky. Sometimes you just happen to luck into things. I never have been so fortunate. Uncle Raffie, just look how lucky you've been!"

I watched as the old man's face turned from expressionlessness to a rigid, stern look. I could sense he was trying to keep a calmness and equanimity in his expression, but he was losing the internal battle. "Listen, José, you have once again insulted me. You can't keep a job, and all you do is ask for money and handouts. I'm tired of supporting you. You quit jobs, drink, and take drugs. I've talked to your mother many times, and she does not know what to do with you. You are hurting your mother."

The nephew's tone became harsher and louder. "Why did you talk to my mother? You don't have a right to do that."

"Yes, I do," Raffie answered, raising his voice. "I am trying to help you and your mother. But you are ungrateful and undisciplined. You've had opportunities, but you just won't work. All you want to do in life is have fun."

"It's not my fault," the nephew answered, "if people don't respect me or try to understand me. You know the world doesn't treat people like me well."

"Yes, the world is a difficult place," Raffie scolded. "Sometimes it doesn't treat people like you and me well. But you have to try. You don't try, José. You are always trying to find a shortcut or a way of getting money without working for it. The world doesn't work that way either."

"Well, if you could just spare me seven or eight hundred, I could get down to Amarillo and get that job. I wouldn't be back here."

Raffie cleared his throat again. "You've said that before. And how many times have you been back looking for a new handout?"

"Things just didn't work out. But I promise you they will this time. I can see this being a great move for me."

Raffie appeared to be totally frustrated and threw his arms in the air to make a point. "You always say this. I want you to understand something. If I give you the money this time, I don't want to see you here again. And you know it hurts me to see what you've done to your mother and the legacy of your father. It really hurts me."

The nephew looked down and seemed to fight back a slow smile. "If I can get the money, I will not need to come back. It will all work out, Uncle Raffie. I know it will."

"I don't believe that for a moment. But this is the last time I will give you money. I suppose you still don't have a bank account?"

The nephew nodded. "Not yet. I will open an account when I get to Amarillo."

Raffie leaned forward and pulled out a folded wad of cash and began counting out eight crisp one-hundred-dollar bills. He was still very angry and annoyed, and he did not look at his nephew as he handed him the money.

The nephew eagerly reached out and took the cash. He smiled slyly and turned and walked away, not responding to his uncle's generosity.

As he walked to his truck, Raffie yelled out after him, "Did you hear me, José? This is the last time. Don't come back asking for more. Please make something of yourself. Make your mother happy."

The nephew climbed into his truck, and after several sputtering-out attempts, the engine finally turned over. He backed up swiftly and, without looking up, peeled off spinning his tires, creating a wisp of smoke.

Once the truck was out of sight, Raffie turned to me and said, "Paul, I'm sorry you had to hear all that."

"I understand that was a tough situation to deal with," I responded.

"Paul, I don't mind helping people who want to be helped. But there are people like my nephew who do not want to work for whatever reason. They may be lazy, or they just give up and want the world to support them."

"I understand. I've worked with people like your nephew," I said. "And I have one in my family as well."

"Paul, I believe most people want to work and feel useful. We just need to be frank with those that don't want to do anything but be victims. They don't realize their problems are almost always self-inflicted. These are the people that don't want to help themselves. You give them your hand, and they try to pull you down with them."

The old man's eyes brightened and opened wider as he spoke. "I see that my nephew ruined his life. But there was and still is so much opportunity around him that he refuses to acknowledge. America is still the land of great opportunities. If you can't make it in this country, I don't think you can make it anywhere. It's hard to say this, but the people on our streets that do drugs and commit crimes and have mental illnesses probably wouldn't be alive in most third world countries. Or they would live an incredibly destitute existence or might even be socked away in some hellish prison for most of their lives."

I thought about what Raffie had just said. But I felt I needed to press a counternarrative on his statements. "Raffie, I agree with most of what you just said there. But I do think society has created obstacles for some members of our society."

The old man rubbed his hands back and forth on the arms of the chair for a moment and then said, "Paul, every society has a class of people like my nephew. A group of people that want life to be easy. But America allows everyone a chance to achieve success based on their abilities. Privilege only goes so far. I think we get these terms confused in America today. Privilege does not guarantee success; abilities and hard work guarantee success. If you are truly good at what you do, the cream will always rise to the top. Look at most of your billionaires today—few were spawned from privileged backgrounds."

"Yeah," I responded. "But some did come from backgrounds of privilege."

"I'm not saying there aren't privileged individuals with generational wealth in America," the old man continued, "but that doesn't prevent anyone in this country from achieving success. Just because someone else inherited wealth or worked hard and achieved financial success doesn't prevent me from doing so as well." The old man cleared his throat and added, "And I think the playing field today is much different than it was a hundred years ago. We seem to forget how far we've come. If you live in the past and you don't think you can be successful in the present, you won't be successful. I still believe great opportunities are achievable today if someone has the right abilities and is willing to work to achieve their goals."

As I listened, Raffie turned toward me to make a salient point. "Paul, the reality of generational wealth is over subsequent generations it often becomes diluted and eventually can be much less for each subsequent generation."

*****

A new, shiny black sedan pulled up between two dilapidated work trucks that were parked in front of us. A rather stately tall man in a dark tailored suit and blue striped tie got out and walked toward us. I was watching him and noticed his hair was perfectly slicked back and coiffured. In all aspects, he could be described as dashing and smooth.

As he stepped up onto the deck, he smiled charmingly at Raffie and greeted him cheerfully, holding his hand out for a handshake. "Hi, I am Roger Adams, and I am running to be your next US Congressman. I am here because I wish to ask for your support, Mr. Raffie. Do you mind if I have a seat here next to you?"

Raffie looked up and shook the smooth gentleman's hand and said pleasantly, "By all means, Mr. Adams. Have a seat."

I watched as the man sat down. He leaned back in the chair and threw his head up in the air as if he was sniffing the air for acceptance. "As I said, I'm running to be your congressman, and I know, Mr. Raffie, that you are a prominent figure in this community. Everyone tells me I need to work through you to gain this community's support."

The old man leaned back in his chair now, and I watched as he ruminated over the politician's words. Then he said, "I am flattered by your words. When you ask me for your support, what do you think I can do for you?"

The politician smiled and quickly responded with what sounded like a well-rehearsed response. "Well, to begin with I need you to promote me in your community, to speak highly of me and encourage others to support me at the voting booth. Tell them that I understand their plight and want to help them. That I personally care about people and their plights in struggling through life."

The old man sighed and said, "So how are you going to help them with their plight?"

"Well, I was hoping to build a resource center where your people can go and get counseling and job training and mental health awareness. This would be a real progressive change for your people and community."

The old man leaned forward and asked, "My people?"

"You know, people that are consistent with your ethnicity. And this facility would be built in the heart of your people's community. It would only be used by your people."

The old man sighed again. "And why not used by all people of every ethnicity that need help with their plights? Doesn't everyone have a right to try to better themselves?"

The politician did not speak at first. He seemed stunned by Raffie's response. He finally responded awkwardly in bewilderment, "Well, uh, I guess…others could use it too. You can't close the doors and only allow one group to use the facility, I suppose. I don't think that would be constitutional. But this facility will benefit your community."

The old man now inquired, "Your name is Adams, right? Weren't you a state senator at one time?"

The politician's face brightened, and he answered cheerfully, "Yes, you are right. I've served you before from the state level. I'm now running at the federal level."

The old man rubbed the back of his neck and said, "Well, I recall our community was promised this facility some time ago by the state. But it was only a promise. What happened? Did you not have any influence over that situation?"

The politician looked down, and the cheerful look on his face gradually dissipated. He now spoke in a serious tone, appearing defensive. "I tried. I honestly tried, but our money ran out. Our money just ran out. You know we have only so much money to work with."

"Your money," Raffie asked. "You own the money?"

"Well, yes," the politician answered. "It's taxes that we have. Once we have it, it is our money to use. We use it as we see fit. And this time we have the land ready to build the center on."

The old man looked at the politician and suddenly admonished him, "Mr. Adams, let me correct you on one point. Your money is the money of the people. You don't have any money. You only have an elected responsibility to be good stewards of the taxpayers' money and to use it wisely and responsibly."

"Well, OK, I suppose," he answered reluctantly. "You could look at it that way. We are managing the money we get through taxes and fees."

"And Mr. Adams, what else do you need from me?" the old man asked, chuckling to himself. "I suppose something financial as well? Surely you came asking for money along with my endorsement."

The politician's cheerful smile returned, and he said sheepishly, "Well, yes, Mr. Raffie, that would help also. Any additional financial support you could provide would help me get more good work done. You know it's very expensive to run a campaign these days. And let me say my opponent is a strong candidate, but I know things about her past I can use. But I still need money to get the word out."

The old man asked, "So you plan on running a negative campaign?"

The politician quickly retorted, "Only a little negative campaigning. You have to differentiate yourself from your competitor. You know, I want to look better versus the competition. You always want to be perceived as the better person."

"Instead of trying to be perceived as the better person, why not run on what you believe as a person? What your policies are? And how your platform policies will truly benefit the community?" the old man asked.

The politician thought for a moment and then responded, "Well, what I believe is what the party believes. My message is wrapped in the party's message and the party's policies. I can only promise what I can promise. But our party is the good party. We want to help everyone."

"But you can't help everyone," Raffie responded. "Let's be realistic. You don't have enough resources to help everyone."

"Yes, but at least we are trying and doing something to help people," the politician interjected. "We are doing good, and we have good policies."

"How do you know you are doing good?" Raffie asked. "I've seen plenty of governmental policies over the years that were sold as good for our country to get votes. But later on, they created unforeseen negative consequences. They actually hurt communities."

The politician paused and then answered in a dismissive tone, "Well, I'm sure that happens every now and then."

Raffie rubbed his chin for a moment and then asked thoughtfully, "By the way, three years ago I gave that parcel of land you speak of to the state to build the job skills and training center. I was told the funds were already set aside to build the center. Again, what happened?"

The politician looked toward his left and answered, "Well, we had to provide some cash subsistence payments to many people who needed the money. So as often happens, money was moved from one bucket into another. It's a matter of prioritizing government expenses."

"So some folks in this community got cash money but no one got a hand up? And I imagine the money was handed out right before elections, right?"

The politician appeared to be deep in thought, trying to recall the time period for the cash distributions. "Well, I don't recall. I will have to go back and check."

I thought about what Raffie had said earlier, that neither party had a monopoly on virtue and truth. That neither party was wholly altruistic, or at least realistic. It was all about obtaining and retaining power. I thought maybe the devices and methods used to achieve and retain power were the ethical and moral issues that should be studied more closely by the voters. And the party platforms should also be studied. The platforms truly differentiate the approaches used to govern and how each party will govern.

"So you think, Mr. Adams, that what you have on your opponent will make you look better?" the old man asked. "That you will be viewed as the better guy?"

The politician sat straight up in his chair now, appearing pious, and replied, "Well, what she did was unacceptable. It could be construed as maybe even illegal. Our party's legal team can help me on that issue. Either way we will paint it as illegal. The public will accept it."

"So this is how you win in politics?" Raffie asked. "'I'm not as bad as my opponent is'? Even if it is not entirely true?"

"No, listen here—this is not wrong, what I'm doing," the politician pleaded. "I am very professional, and I have been told I come across looking very sincere and honest. If people don't know about my opponent, the wrong person could win the election."

"Hmmm," the old man pondered. "So again, it gets down to a popularity contest? 'I am a better person than my opponent, so vote for me.' You don't push what you personally believe in, and you always toe the party line. And you promise things to get votes, using tax revenues that are not yours. And since you are talking to me for your support, you also source votes by targeting specific ethnic community leaders who you think should support you blindly."

The politician hesitated and then responded with a growing level of curtness. "Well, that's the way it's always been. I am no different from anyone else running for office. And now I suppose you won't support me? That is a shame if that happens."

The old man looked the slick politician in the eye and said, "Not until I hear the platforms from both parties will I endorse anyone. I don't give my resources to candidates running on popularity. Look, Mr. Adams, you may be a good guy, but I don't know what you stand for. And I don't know if your policies are too idealistic or if they will even work. And even given all that, I don't know if you can fulfill them."

"Well, fine, then," the politician abruptly answered. "It looks like I'm not winning you over today. So there's no reason I should stay here any longer. I should just go right now!"

The old man smiled and said, "That's up to you, Mr. Adams."

I watched as the politician stood up and dusted the back of his suit off. He then turned toward the street and marched down the steps back to his sleek black car.

As he drove off, Raffie turned to me and scoffed, "Politicians and political parties! They'll do anything to obtain and stay in power. They will ultimately be the undoing and downfall of our country."

*****

I heard a voice calling my name. I looked up and saw Diego across the street waving his arms and motioning for me to come over to his garage. My car was still sitting outside Diego's in front of one of the large garage bays. Even at this late hour in the afternoon, the sun reflected off the windshield, shooting blinding rays of light in all directions.

I got up slowly and turned toward Raffie. He was sitting and contentedly looking across the highway at Diego. I rubbed the back of my head slowly, feeling exhausted. This had been a very long day so far, and there was still more to come. I had a three-hour drive ahead of me to get to the Albuquerque airport. And after that I had a three-hour flight home.

I stood on the deck for a moment, thinking about how to say goodbye to Raffie. I looked at the old man, and I felt both admiration and some sympathy toward him. The old man seemed lonely in the twilight of his life. And yet he was fully alive and engaged in the world about him. He did not attempt to be a progenitor of any movement or profess to be swayed by any cognoscenti's beliefs. Again, I had never met anyone quite like him. He was kind, firm, caring, and fair to people. He wasn't judgmental, and he possessed an overwhelming sense of optimism in a world of naysayers. He sincerely felt that everyone should be respected and appreciated for their hard work and contributions to society. He loved this country, and he was proud to have served this country. He was a model citizen and a strong supporter of common sense, and he was truly guided by his faith. Many people profess to know what a true American is today, but for me Raffie exemplified all the positive attributes of a true American.

I suddenly felt that my affection toward this old man could not end today. Would I ever meet anyone like Raffie again in my life? How many Raffies were left in this country? With his generation's passing, would America's persona end, doused and extinguished like a candle? As easy as it was to enter into Raffie's world and be accepted as a confidant and friend, I would be departing now, and probably I would never see him again. We were like the proverbial two ships that passed each other at just this one moment in time and space. Yet our discussions I would internalize, and I felt they would stay with me the rest of my life. And maybe I could somehow mimic and adopt his approaches to life and achieve just a portion of the satisfaction and fulfillment he experienced.

I reached down to shake his hand. He raised his arm with some effort and grasped my hand. His handshake was strong and firm.

"It was a pleasure to talk to you today, Raffie." I fumbled for words. "I also want to thank you for the sandwiches and drinks." I felt suddenly that this farewell was just not sufficient. My good-bye to Raffie needed to have much more substance and genuineness— not just the normal casual good-bye.

Before I could speak again, Raffie looked up at me and said, "Paul, you're welcome. It was a pleasure to talk to you today. I hope you have a safe trip home. I wish you and your family the best in life. God bless."

Still feeling my farewell was insufficient, I replied, "Raffie, I appreciate your advice and words of wisdom today. If I pass this way again, I promise I will stop here and spend a day with you, if that's OK."

The old man looked tired as he sat there bent over in the chair. He smiled slowly, and with a genuine wink he said, "Paul, that would be good. I would be happy to see you again. I must confess that today is an unusual day. Usually things are pretty quiet around here. Hopefully I did not bore you today. Tomorrow, I might be sitting here with someone who may not be as patient with me." He looked down at his watch and said, "You were here a long time today. And it is getting late. I'll be heading home as well shortly. I wish you safe travels the rest of the day. And if you are ever in this area again, yes, please stop by."

I offered, "Can I at least give you a ride home?"

"No, I will be all right."

As I turned away, I ended by saying, "Raffie, thank you and take care."

*****

Diego met me with a broad smile and ushered me over to my rental car. He gave me an invoice, and I studied it for a moment. I folded the invoice and put it in my pocket. After paying Diego inside his garage and thanking him, I climbed into the rental car. I slowly drove up onto the highway in the fading light of the afternoon. The evening would be fast approaching, and with it the temperature would begin dropping.

I looked across the street now at Miggy's. The chairs on the front porch were deserted. The car moved forward and slowly accelerated on the smooth black pavement. Just as I reached the point where that day's accident had occurred, I saw a bent figure plodding heavily along the dusty shoulder of the road.

ABOUT THE AUTHOR

Robert H. Higel, a seasoned professional in Banking and Finance, brings his profound insight to his novel, Sage of Las Cruces. Graduating from the University of Florida with an Accounting Business Administration degree, he later added a Masters in Business Administration from the University of Tampa to his academic accolades. As a Certified Public Accountant, he held esteemed roles such as Chief Financial Officer and Chief Operating Officer in numerous banks over forty-five years. A life-long follower of political and social trends, Higel channels his understanding into creating a simple yet compelling dialogue in his novel.

Milton Keynes UK
Ingram Content Group UK Ltd.
UKHW030949181124
451360UK00006B/768